SHOE WARS

BY Liz Pichon
(who likes shoes not WAR.)

SCHOLASTIC

This shoe book belongs to:

Published in the UK by Scholastic, 2021
Euston House, 24 Eversholt Street, London, NW1 1DB
Scholastic Ireland, 89E Lagan Road, Dublin Industrial Estate,
Glasnevin, Dublin, D11 HP5F

SCHOLASTIC and associated logos are trademarks and/or
registered trademarks of Scholastic Inc.

ISBN 978 1407 19110 2

A CIP catalogue record for this book is available from the British Library.

Printed by CPI Group (UK) Ltd, Croydon, CR0 4YY
Paper made from wood grown in sustainable forests and other controlled sources.

1 3 5 7 9 10 8 6 4 2

www.scholastic.co.uk

For
MARK

(Happy 30th
anniversary!)

♥ ✕✕✕

SHOE·PID·I·TY

Wearing shoes that don't fit.

Who knew?

Best Foot
Forward

T here's an old saying that goes something like THIS:

You can tell a LOT about a person from the shoes they're wearing...

Random wise person

Do you think that's true?

Take a look at your own

shoes right now.

What do they say about YOU?

Do you like **sport?**

Maybe you enjoy *relaxing*.

O r were you just late for school and got **con***fus***e***d*?

Because some shoes are NOT what they seem to be...

Here are two pairs of shoes.

(Both feature a lot in this story.)

PAIR A have BIG, BULGINg EYES, menacing metal spikes, a W I D E, gaping mouth crammed full of *sharp teeth* and, if anything gets too close, sensors that ROAR. These shoes look scary. And if you wore them, you'd definitely stand out in a crowd, *that's* for sure.

PAIR B is a nice, neat, flat shoe, the kind you might wear for school, because teachers LOVE a sensible shoe, don't they? These are practical shoes, if a bit dull.

SO, the IMPORTANT QUESTION is:

Which pair would YOU choose if you found yourself

in THIS situation? ⟶

Imagine you're walking down a street, whistling a **jolly tune.**

(If you can't whistle, *SING.*)

SUDDENLY, you hear a dog barking LOUDLY.

You turn around, and it's running towards you,

and NOT in a friendly, tickle-my-tummy way. The closer the

dog gets, the angrier it looks – and I mean **FIERCE.** Its teeth

glisten with dog drool that's flying out of its MOUTH!

Your first thought is: **GET AWAY!**

As fast as you can before it's too late!

(It is too late, by the way.)

Grrr

The dog is already at your heels and growling.

You hold your breath and keep absolutely still, hoping it doesn't

want to bite you.

(It does want to bite you.)

The dog narrows its eyes and begins to move closer.

It's getting ready to LEAP UP

and sink its TEETH right into

your BIG ...

rrrrrrr JUICY ...

... WAIT!

Let's STOP everything right there for a second.

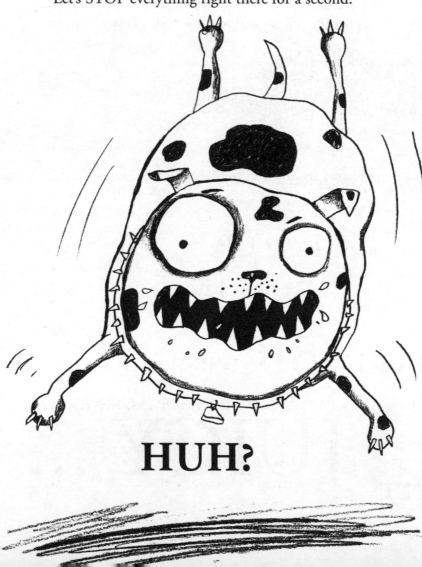

HUH?

If you had to pick one pair of shoes to PROTECT **your** feet

from the VICIOUS DOG, which shoes would YOU choose?

PAIR A: or **PAIR B:**

the SCARY-LOOKING the SENSIBLE-LOOKING
SHOES SHOES

In case you need it, here's some more thinking time:

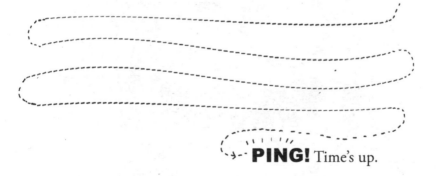

PING! Time's up.

Did you pick PAIR A, the **SCARY-LOOKING SHOES**, the

ones with the metal spikes, SHARP teeth and the sensors?

Then you'd be COMPLETELY and utterly …

... **wrong!** And here's why.

Firstly, they belong to someone called

Wendy Wedge, and if you pinched her shoes, she'd

be FURIOUS!

Wendy would send out one of her MEAN, crazy dogs

to get them back.

Secondly, **JUST LOOK AT THEM!**

They're spiky, clumpy, weird and wobbly. WHO

could even walk, let alone RUN in a pair of shoes like that?

(Apart from Wendy Wedge, of course.)

BUT if you picked **PAIR B?**

Well, these shoes might not

look like anything special, but they really are.

All you'd have to do to ESCAPE Wendy's dog is click your

heels together and say,

"SHOES UP!"

Then **WHOOOOSSSSSHHHH!**

Off you'd go like a ROCKET, and the dog would be left

wondering where you were and biting on nothing but air,

because these shoes can FLY!

(HOW exciting is that?)

Imagine the FUN you could have wearing flying shoes.

You'd never be late for school again.

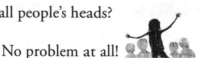

Reaching anything high would be EASY!

Looking over tall people's heads?

No problem at all!

Flying shoes would be **AMAZING.**

EVERYONE would want a pair (including me).

But... (There's always a "but", isn't there?)

Before you get too excited about the shoes, the person who owns

them doesn't want ANYONE to know they even EXIST.

ESPECIALLY not one person in particular:

Wendy  Wedge.

(Yes, HER again.)

Because if SHE finds out about the shoes, it would be a

DISASTER!

First, Wendy would STEAL the shoes. Then she would LIE and

say that SHE invented them. Then being a **NASTY** piece of work,

she'd USE them to ENTER the MOST prestigious competition

EVER

— THE GOLDEN SHOE AWARD.

(Wendy Wedge is so desperate to win, it's painful.)

Every FOUR years the VERY BEST shoemaking towns are

INVITED to compete for the **ultimate** SHOE prize.

At the BIG, *GLITZY* ceremony, the competition is always FIERCE. The most inventive and incredible shoes with gadgets are presented to the panel of judges.

THE GOLDEN SHOE AWARD

A winning pair of shoes can change the fortunes AND lives of the inventors **FOR EVER.**

So far, this has NOT happened to Wendy Wedge.

She enters every single competition. But she's only won a prize once, for **BEST COMEDY SHOE ...**

and even that was a mistake.

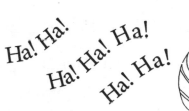

Ha! Ha! Ha! Ha! Ha! Ha! Ha!

It's not like Wendy hasn't tried to win

THE GOLDEN SHOE AWARD.

Her brand of clunky, thick WEDGES just haven't impressed

the judges.

But with a pair of FLYING SHOES, the top **AWARD**

would be HERS, and no one could laugh at her ever again.

Wendy would become even MORE

powerful and VILE than she is now, and

WHO KNOWS what other dastardly

deeds she'd get up to?

So you understand why keeping these shoes hidden is REALLY

important. And so far they've been a VERY

well-kept secret. Right up until now...

...when EVERYGHING is about to change.

(The dog's still fine, in case you were worried.

Look at its happy little face.)

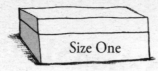

Size One

SHOE TOWN was famous for one thing

... melons. (I'm joking – it's shoes, of course.)

Ivor Foot lived there with his two children, **Ruby** and **Bear,** on

the **Shoebox Estate** in a small house that was shaped like – you

guessed it – a shoebox.

One night, when most people on the estate were fast asleep, a

slightly odd sound began to *WAFT* out of the Foot family's house.

It was a sort of…

WHOOSH whooosh WHOOSHING noise...

It woke Ruby up.

She was used to hearing noises what with all the shoebox houses

being so close together, but for some reason this felt different and

she wasn't sure why.

Ruby kept listening.

WHOOooooSHhhhh
WHOOOoooSH
WHOOSHHHHH

There it was again.

"Bear... BEAR!" Ruby called

out to her brother, who was sleeping on the other

side of the room they shared. He didn't answer, so Ruby got up.

Bear could sleep through anything, which Ruby found annoying.

"BEAR, did you hear that?" Ruby gave him a good shake.

"I'm asleep," he grumbled.

"No, you're not," Ruby pointed out.

"I am," Bear mumbled and turned over.

"Bear..." Ruby kept SHAKING him.

"Go back to bed," Bear told her.

Then the NOISE happened again.

WHOOooooSHhhhh
WHOOOoooSH
WHOOSHHHHH

"What is it?" Ruby asked, leaning over him.

"Probably a ... monster," Bear told her wearily.

"Funny. I'm going to get Dad up," Ruby said.

"Don't wake Dad," Bear sighed, but Ruby ignored him

   (she did that a lot).

She slid open their bedroom door and saw light coming from the

kitchen.

Good, Dad's already awake, Ruby thought to herself. But it

sounded like someone else was with him. She could hear talking.

Who was it?

Ruby crept down the hallway, stepping over the creaky bits on the floor. Then she hid behind the bookcase (her secret place to listen to grown-up chats without being seen).

Pushing a thick cookery book over to one side left a nice gap for her to peer into the kitchen. She could hear Dad talking, but she couldn't see him.

"That's enough excitement for one night.

Come on, Shoo, let's get you down."

Ruby smiled. So THAT'S what the noise was!

It was Shoo, their cat, who often got STUCK on top of the cupboard. Dad must be rescuing her.

THEN, out of the corner of her eye, Ruby saw something

floating down from the ceiling. She looked up … and blinked a few

times. Was she seeing things?

"Whooooaaa…"

Her mouth

dropped open.

TWO FEET

were hovering

in the air.

Then slowly,

they began

to drop

down,

lower

and

lower

and

lower.

IT WAS DAD!

BUT IT was the **SHOES** he was wearing that

REALLY got Ruby's attention.

On either side of each shoe was a small white feathered wing that

was fluttering up and down and making THAT

WHOOooooSHing
WHOOOooooSH
whooooshing noise.

Ruby stared as Dad brought the shoes down to land.

She wanted to SHOUT,

"DAD! YOU'VE GOT
FLYING SHOES!"

She'd NEVER seen flying shoes before.

No one had.

They were supposed to be *impossible* to make.

As Dad got closer to the ground, he

SUDDENLY began to

LURCH *one way*

and then the other.

Then his feet began to **wobble,**

and

SWAY ...

from side ...

... to side.

"Oooopppps! Come on, shoes,

not now.

Shoes DOWN!

Shoes DOWN!

Easy does it."

Finally, her dad got things under control and landed safely.

"Rescue complete," he declared as Shoo leaped from his arms

on to the floor. Ruby rubbed her eyes. WAS THIS REALLY

HAPPENING? She had a million questions to ask Dad like:

Did you MAKE the flying shoes?

How high can they fly?

Can I get my OWN pair?

How FAST do they go?

And MOST importantly,

WHY HAVE YOU BEEN KEEPING

THE FLYING SHOES SECRET?!

Ruby was about to come out from behind the

bookshelves to get answers when something

Dad said instantly STOPPED her.

"REMEMBER, Shoo, NO ONE can EVER find out about these

flying shoes.

NOT Ruby,

NOT Bear

and, MOST IMPORTANTLY,

NOT WENDY WEDGE!"

Ruby froze.

Wendy Wedge was her dad's horrible boss and Ruby didn't

like her at all (not many people did).

Dad sounded serious.

"If Wendy Wedge EVER got her

hideous hands on, or horrible feet in,

these shoes, it would be a DISASTER."

Mine all mine!

FLYING SHOE

Dad paused and shivered.

"She'd fly into a FURY. She'd STEAL the shoes from me and she'd take everything else I own – AGAIN! Nothing's safe from Wendy Wedge, not even YOU," Dad said and pointed at Shoo.

Ruby gulped.

It was too late – she'd already seen the shoes.

I'm good at keeping secrets. I won't tell anyone, Ruby thought.

Although she might have to tell Bear

(if he was nice to her).

She stayed very still and tried to listen some more.

"You know what? With a bit more work, I reckon we

COULD WIN **THE GOLDEN SHOE AWARD**

with these. Imagine the look on Wendy's face,"

Dad said, taking a deep breath in.

"It was always Sally's DREAM to win the award

with flying shoes. She invented them when we owned

the shop, and worked on the plans for years until they

were almost perfect."

He shook his head.

"If it hadn't been for that snake, things would

be so different.

I wouldn't be working for **Wendy Wedge**, THAT'S for sure."

Shoo *meowed* like she was answering Dad back.

Ruby kept quiet. She missed her mum too.

Ruby and Bear had been very young when their mother died

from a ***poisonous* snakebite.** It was a total mystery where

the snake had come from and no one knew where it had slithered

off to. Sally's death had made the news, as snakes had never been

seen before in **SHOE TOWN.**

Sally Sandal (Ruby and Bear's mum) when she made shoes.

Ruby's mum and dad had run a shoe shop together that sold

Sally's amazing inventions. They all lived above the shop. But after

Sally died, Dad got sad  and stopped making any shoes or

running the shop. His good friends Betty Boot and Bert

I brought a casserole

Brogue had tried their very best to

help out, but nothing could STOP Wendy

Wedge from *SWOOPING* in like a VULTURE

to make Dad an offer it was hard to refuse.

"Sell me your shop and everything in it,

and I'll give you a job at World of

Wedge, and a house on the Shoebox

Estate too, because I am a very good

person* and I CARE DEEPLY about you and your family," she'd

told him. **"Think of your CHILDREN, Ivor. Sign here and ALL**

your problems will DISAPPEAR."

Wendy had lied.

*Foot note: Wendy is not a good person.

The contract was **MASSIVE** with a LOT of conditions written in tiny teeny writing.

Dad was in a terrible position. He needed the money badly and didn't feel like he had a choice.

"We need time to pack. I'm keeping everything Sally made," Dad had insisted. Then, with Wendy's grizzly dogs growling around his feet, Dad had reluctantly signed.

SIGN HERE

Ivor Foot

The family had only just moved out

when Wendy arranged for the whole shoe shop

... to be knocked down.

Luckily, Ivor had managed to rescue the FLYING SHOES and

keep them safely away from Wendy. Those shoes had become even

MORE precious to Ivor now that he no longer had his wonderful

Sally, his sole mate, by his side. He was determined to keep them

safe, along with her books and a few other possessions.

Now, Ivor glanced at the clock. It was after 2:30 a.m. He began

putting the shoes away in their wooden box.

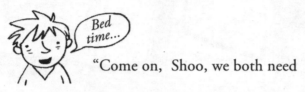

"Come on, Shoo, we both need

to get some rest," he said.

"That's enough excitement for one night. Let's go check on

the kids and make sure they're still asleep."

Ruby gulped.

"Uh-oh..."

She had to go **NOW** before Dad saw

her, and there wasn't much time.

Ruby slid out from behind the bookcase and quickly tiptoed down the hall, avoiding the creaky floorboards back to her room, where Bear was still asleep and snoring quietly.

zzzzz

zzz

Ruby **jumped** under the covers and pulled them over her head. She was followed closely by Shoo, who then decided it was a good idea to

L E A P on to Ruby's bed and start pressing her paws UP and DOWN like she was kneading dough.

"Geroff me, Shoo!" Ruby hissed, but Shoo wouldn't budge.

SHOO!

Ruby pretended to be asleep as Dad came in. He checked Bear was OK, then walked over to Ruby and gently lifted Shoo up. Ruby stayed very still and didn't move.

"Night, night, Ruby and Bear. Sleep tight, don't wear your shoes too tight," Dad whispered, then carried Shoo out and slid the door shut.

Ruby waited for a few seconds before she breathed OUT and her EYES pinged WIDE open. HOW could she go to sleep NOW?

All she could think about was ... **FLYING SHOES.**

Flying shoes with white feather wings!

Flying shoes flying up and down.

Dad had flying shoes!

Should she tell Bear? Or would he BLAB?

It was supposed to be a secret after all.

Her mind was BUZZING, but it was so late that slowly her eyes

began to get heavier ... and heavier ... and heavier.

Until ...

flying ... shoes...

shoes ... flying shoes ...

chocolate ... choco ... late...

Flying
Chocolate

Mmmmmmmmm.

Zzzzzzzzzzzzzzz
Zzzzzzzzzzz

35

 Size Two

"**W**akey, Wakey!"

Bear leaned over Ruby and gave her a little shake.

He was already dressed and ready for school.

"I'm awake," she told him, groaning.

"It's annoying when someone wakes you up,

isn't it?" Bear smirked.

Ruby sat bolt upright as she remembered –

 the FLYING SHOES!

"You look like a zombie. That's what happens when you get up in

the night," Bear said and *PRODDED* her, which was ANNOYING.

Without thinking, Ruby replied, "WELL, YOU missed out by

NOT getting up, because I saw…"

"What?" asked Bear.

"Err, nothing," said Ruby.

Bear pulled a face at her.

"You saw … A **MONSTER!**"

he roared, trying to make her jump.

"Funny," Ruby said, glaring at him and NOT laughing.

"OK. I'll just ask Dad."

"No, don't!" she shouted.

Bear looked at her carefully.

"What are you hiding, Ruby?"

"Nothing, I just need to get ready for school.

And if you don't stop BUGGING me, I'll sing your

FAVOURITE song."

"DON'T SING!"

Bear covered his ears.

Singing was Ruby's secret weapon to annoy him.

"Too late!" she shouted and BURST into song.

"Chips! What do we want?

We want CHIPS!

When do we want them? Now!"

Bear put his hands over his ears.

"That stupid SONG will be STUCK in my head all

day now," he said and stomped out of the room.

Ruby stopped singing and sighed. She knew there was no

way Bear would let this go. He never forgot anything. Bear had

an amazing memory for all kinds of weird facts, odd things and

peculiar creatures.

She pulled the lever to open up her wardrobe and the clothes rail

shot out. It was messy but Ruby knew where everything was.

The whole of their house was filled with all kinds of unusual space-saving gadgets and quirky bits of furniture: chairs that turned into tables, tables that pulled out from walls and shelves that spun around to become pictures.

SWOOSH

Over the years their dad had made ordinary objects EXTRAORDINARY and nothing was what it seemed to be.

It was a small house, but what it lacked in space it made up for in style, **imagination** and colour, everywhere.

Ruby got dressed and pulled the lever again.

Her clothes rail glided back into the box with a nice

satisfying **Swoooshhhhing** sound.

She grabbed her school bag and pretended

to skate her way to the kitchen in her socks.

Bear and Dad were having breakfast at the table. The top

was covered in Mum's hand-painted tiles and each tile showed a

different shoe from their old shop on it – the sorts of shoes not easy

to find in **SHOE TOWN** any more.

There were comfy cloud shoes, shoes that

looked like sandwiches with a secret

compartment to keep snacks in, super-WHIZZY shoes with wheels

and lights, useful shoes with storage

drawers in the heels,

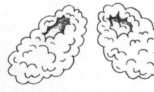

and pencil shoes with some handy notepaper attached. There were

even fish-shaped shoes.

No wedges, though.

Ruby noticed that Dad looked more tired than usual. (She knew why.)

"Morning, Ruby. Did you sleep OK?" he asked her.

Before she could answer, Bear interrupted.

"Nope. Ruby woke ME up and then she wanted to wake YOU

up too, Dad."

"No, I didn't!" Ruby protested.

"Were you awake last night?" Dad asked her.

"I thought I heard a noise, but it was just Bear snoring." Ruby

shrugged like it was nothing.

ZZZZZ

"I don't snore…" Bear told her.

"You so DO – like a WARTHOG."

Ruby snorted to show him what he sounded like.

"Ha! That sounds more like ME!" Dad laughed then cleared his

throat. "Hey, listen, you two. I've got a surprise for you. BUT you

have to **PROMISE** me that you won't tell anyone. It has to be

our secret."

Ruby sat up and paid attention. Was Dad going to tell them

about the flying shoes?

"What is it, Dad?" Bear asked.

"Well, it's about the NEW school shoes you all have to wear

now."

Ruby and Bear groaned.

"Wendy calls them her WOWs – that's World of Wedge

shoes."

"Ugh. World Of STUPID SHOES more like.

Why can't we wear USEFUL shoes to school like THESE?"

Bear pointed to the WHIZZY lights and wheeled shoes on

the table tiles.

"Or cloud shoes. They'd be all FLUFFY

and SO comfy!" Ruby agreed.

"I know these WOWs aren't

very comfortable—"

"You can say that again," Bear interrupted, grumbling.

"WOWs should stand for Worst Ordinary Wobbly shoes –

ever. AND they're really hard to run around in too," he added.

"I'm sorry guys, it's the school rules," Dad continued. "But I

knew you wouldn't be happy about wearing them, so I've made a

few TWEAKS, even though I'm not supposed to."

Ruby and Bear stopped eating and looked at each

other in excitement.

"Wait here, I'll be right back," Dad said.

As soon as he left, Ruby turned to Bear and whispered,

"I know what Dad's done to our school shoes."

"What?" he asked.

"Last night, when I woke up I saw something AMAZING."

"Did you?"

"YES! Dad was in the kitchen, and you'll NEVER guess what he

was wearing…" She paused to make her brother wait a little longer.

"Tell me!" Bear demanded.

"GUESS!"

"Ruby!" Bear sighed.

"Flying shoes! Isn't that FANTASTIC?!"

Bear stared at her suspiciously. "Are you sure?" he asked.

"YES! IT'S TRUE! Dad was flying around the kitchen

UP in the AIR."

Ruby clapped her hands together and made Shoo jump.

"Ruby – everyone knows flying shoes don't ACTUALLY exist. Even Dad said that. It's a FACT. LOTS of people have tried to create them over the years, but everyone's failed," Bear told her. "The last town who tried to enter **THE GOLDEN SHOE AWARD** with flying shoes was Shoecastle. Their synchronized flying team didn't even get off the ground."

Not flying

Ruby shrugged. "Well, Mum managed to do it and Dad has been keeping them a secret from Wendy Wedge all this time."

"I suppose that makes sense. She IS really mean." Bear nodded thoughtfully.

"SO, when Dad comes back we HAVE to act surprised, like we had NO idea he's turned our boring old school shoes into flying shoes, OK?"

Bear nodded. "OK – how's this then?"

He did a SURPRISED face.

"Not bad," said Ruby. "Maybe a bit over the top."

"Or this?" Bear tried again.

"Better," she grinned, just as

Dad came back holding their NEW, IMPROVED school

shoes. That looked exactly the same as the old ones.

Ruby and Bear put on their innocent "we know

nothing" faces.

"What have you done, Dad?" Bear asked.

"Just a few little CHANGES. You don't want to attract any

attention, remember?" Dad said.

"I'm good at keeping secrets!" Ruby smiled.

Bear gave her a look, unconvinced.

"WHAT? I am!" she muttered.

"Now here's what you need to do," said Dad.

Ruby turned to Bear and mouthed the word "FLY" at him.

"There's a secret pad inside each shoe

and if you SCRUNCH UP all your toes

together…" Dad began to explain.

"Yes?" they chorused excitedly.

"At exactly the same time…"

"Yes?" they said again.

"You'll be able to …"

(… *FLY!* Ruby was thinking.)

"... trigger the EXTRA-SQUISHY inner soles that will mould

to your feet and make your shoes SO comfy. Its special fluffiness

makes you feel like you're walking on AIR," Dad told them both.

"Oh." Ruby couldn't hide her disappointment. "Err. Is there

anything else they can do, Dad?" she asked hopefully.

"Just a few more things.

THIS bit's really good,

if I do say so myself.

You need to lean back

on your heels. Right one first, then the left. That activates a

HEATING pad for the cold winter days," Dad told them, hoping

they'd be pleased.

"Um," said Ruby. "Anything else?"

"Oh YES! How could I forget.

You can also ..."

(FLY! FLY! FLY!)

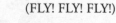

"BOUNCE really high. I've put special springs inside to make every step you take extra bouncy. It's good for running. Just don't overdo it," Dad told them.

Ruby and Bear stared at each other and then at the shoes.

"Is that all?" Ruby said.

"Don't you like the changes?" Dad looked at them, confused.

"We do!" Bear said. "It's just I got really excited because Ruby told me you'd added—"

"WHEELS!" Ruby shouted,

cutting Bear off.

"NO, not WHEELS. You said—"

"LIGHTS! I REALLY WANTED SHOES THAT

LIGHT UP!" She GLARED at Bear to

make him STOP talking.

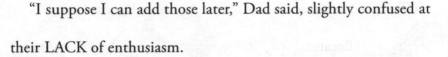

"I suppose I can add those later," Dad said, slightly confused at

their LACK of enthusiasm.

"Thanks, Dad, they're great," Ruby told him.

"Right," Dad said, standing up. "You two go and brush

your teeth. I'll get my work things."

As soon as they were out of earshot, Bear turned to Ruby.

"WHAT was that about? WHY did you keep talking over me?"

"Because I was wrong. Dad didn't make flying shoes for US."

"Obviously," Bear said with a sigh.

"PLEASE don't tell him I saw him flying? Not yet," Ruby begged.

"And did you? Really?" Bear asked.

"YES!" Ruby snapped. "If you don't believe me, I'll prove it. The shoes must be HERE in the house somewhere."

"Why can't we just ask Dad about them?" Bear suggested.

"Because I HEARD him say 'Ruby and Bear must NEVER find out about the flying shoes.' So please don't say anything, OK?"

"All right, I won't." Bear lowered his voice. "Besides, I might even know where Dad keeps them. He's got a hidden workshop."

"Where? Go on, tell me. I can keep a secret!" Ruby pleaded.

"You really can't."

"Pinky promise…" said Ruby, holding out her little finger to Bear.

"OK. I'll show you after school," he agreed.

They linked their little fingers together and did a pinky promise just as Dad came back and saw them.

"What are you two up to?"

"Just making sure we don't say ANYTHING about our new shoes," Ruby said quickly.

"Good thinking. I like a pinky promise. After all, we don't need any trouble* at school, do we?" Dad said cheerfully.

"As if we'd get into any trouble, Dad," Bear said, looking him STRAIGHT in the eye.

"That would NEVER happen, Dad," Ruby added enthusiastically.

*Foot note: Trouble was coming.

Size Three

Dad, Ruby and Bear left the house together.

Ruby and Bear were finding their new school shoes more fun

than they'd expected. They might not fly,

but BOY could they **bounce.**

"Dad, these shoes

are SO GOOD!"

Ruby told him as she bounced

up and down.

"Easy, you two, we don't want them getting too much attention,"

Dad said, trying to get them to calm down. He could already see

that Mrs Court from across the road was heading their way. She'd

recently moved to the estate so no one knew much about her. But

every time anyone left the house, Mrs Court would APPEAR in an

instant – like she'd been waiting for them.

Mrs Court wore bright **red** winged glasses that matched her bright **red** lipstick, and her dark hair was piled up in a BUN on top of her head.

She used a walking stick to help her get around and for other things too, like pushing open

her gate, shooing away birds and knocking on people's doors.

Right now, Mrs Court was standing in front of them tapping her neat court shoes on the ground.

She didn't look happy.

"Good morning, Mrs Court.

Have you settled in?" Ivor asked politely.

"Mr Foot, there were some odd

NOISES coming from your house last

night. It was very, very late," Mrs Court told him, frowning.

"Are you SURE it was our house? We were all fast asleep, weren't

we, kids?" Ivor said quickly.

He took a step forward, but Mrs Court stuck out her walking

stick to block their way.

"Mr Foot, SOMETHING was going on. I didn't move here to

be disturbed by noisy neighbours."

"I quite understand," Dad said, soothingly.

"Well, I must get to work. And these two need to be at school.

It's a busy day today." He smiled and tried to edge past.

But Mrs Court hadn't finished.

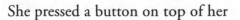

She pressed a button on top of her

walking stick and a sharp point appeared from the end.

"Whoaa…" Ruby was impressed.

Mrs Court then proceeded to SPEAR some dead leaves from the

ground with a quick jabbing movement.

Once she'd collected them, she pressed the

button again and PINGED the leaves OFF

into a nearby bin.

"I don't like MESS," Mrs Court told them.

"MESS was never a problem back in Shoehampton."

"Mess can be a problem in our house!" Ivor joked.

Mrs Court looked at Ivor suspiciously.

"I didn't realize you were from Shoehampton,

Mrs Court. The winners of **THE GOLDEN**

SHOE AWARD for the last three years. You could give

Wendy Wedge a few tips on how to win," Ivor laughed.

"I've heard she can be a very *difficult* person," Mrs Court replied

slowly, peering over her glasses.

"You could say that," Dad agreed.

"She just did, Dad," Ruby pointed out.

"Which is why we must go! I don't want to be late for work,"

Ivor said and turned to leave.

Mrs Court lifted her walking stick up and tapped it three times

on the ground. The stick shrunk into her hand until it was

half its size, then she popped it in her handbag.

Mrs Court strolled back into her house, and called over her shoulder,

"No more noise, please, Mr Foot. I like peace and quiet, remember."

Dad waved. "Lovely to talk to you, Mrs Court," he muttered.

"It wasn't that lovely," Bear mumbled.

"She's tricky," Ruby whispered. "Her stick was awesome, though. I'd like one of those," she told Bear as they watched Mrs Court close her door.

"Come on, kids, let's go. I've got to impress **Wendy** with the wedges I've been working on for **THE GOLDEN SHOE AWARD.** Today is the big presentation and we're all under pressure, so I can't be late."

"The camera wedges you made are THE BEST, Dad! I loved playing with them," Ruby told him.

"You PLAYED with them?"

Dad sounded surprised.

"A little bit…" Ruby said.

"Bear and I both did. They were fun! Dad, if Wendy doesn't like those wedges, she's a twit!" That made Dad laugh.

"They were really excellent, Dad. Wendy would be STUPID not to pick yours," Bear added.

"Well, I just hope **Wendy** likes them as much as you guys do. She's hard to please."

"I don't like Wendy Wedge," Ruby scowled.

"Shhhhhhh! Keep your voice down, you never know who's listening," Dad whispered. He looked up at the HUGE W-shaped building that cast an eerie shadow over the WHOLE of their estate.

"Come on, let's go," Ivor said with a shiver.

As they walked quickly past one of the many HUGE posters around **SHOE TOWN** for **THE GOLDEN SHOE AWARD,** Dad stopped to give Ruby and Bear a last reminder.

"So remember – not a word about your special gadget school shoes.

As far as you're concerned, they're just PLAIN, ordinary shoes and there's nothing unusual about them at all."

Ivor hugged them both and watched as they bounced into school.

I'm higher than you.

LOOK! I'm BOUNCING.

"YOU TWO! STOP BOUNCING!" Ivor called out, then turned towards the BIG gates of the WOW building. Ivor knew it was going to be a difficult day, and he allowed himself a moment to imagine how furious Wendy would be if she knew about Sally's flying shoes, and that cheered him up.

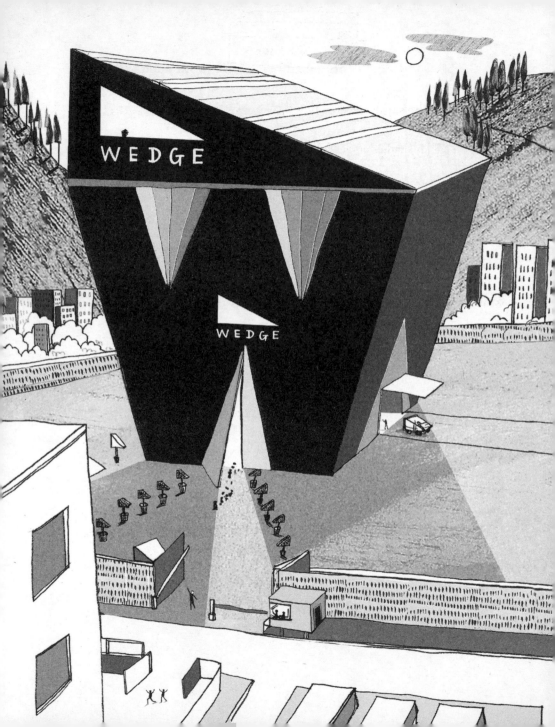

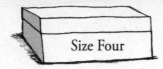

Size Four

At exactly the same time as Ivor was going into WOW, Walter Wedge (Wendy's rather unpleasant son) was walking out.

He was NOT smiling (nothing NEW there).

Walter stomped towards the school accompanied by Wendy's assistant, Mr Creeper, who didn't look happy either. Ruby and Bear were forced to stand back as Walter pushed past.

Walter Wedge was Wendy's only son and not very nice at all. (That's putting it mildly.)

Walter's idea of having fun was to RUIN everyone else's. And if you think I'm exaggerating, this is what he's been up to in just the last few days:

(There's not enough time to tell you EVERYTHING, but you'll get the idea.)

Pushed a boy's ice cream into his face;

helped himself to another kid's toys, then

broke them on purpose; CRUSHED UP  crisps in

their packets, just for FUN;

kicked a football over a high wall

to spoil a game;

ruined a kid's birthday party (that he WASN'T invited to)

by popping the balloons, tipping water over

the cake, helping himself to the food

and, worst of all ...

OPENING the presents!

Does Walter EVER get told off?

NO. Or hardly ever. Once, his mother got cross when he ruined

a pair of her FAVOURITE wedges,

but that was a long time ago.

Walter discovered that the naughtier he was, the more attention his mother gave him. So he just kept on doing it. NO ONE was allowed to say a BAD word about Walter, especially not in front of Wendy. She was such an important and powerful person in **Shoe Town** that people were careful not to upset her. Everyone just put up with Walter's rotten behaviour.

Wendy and Walter were known around town as the gruesome twosome. (Not to their faces – OBVIOUSLY.) When Walter was small, Wendy decided he was far too clever to mix with any other children, so she hired tutors to teach him at home. But thanks to Walter's AWFUL attitude, none of the teachers EVER stayed for long. I mean, why would they? What right-minded teacher would put up with being SOAKED by a bucket of water sneakily placed on top of the door? Or being given a delicious, red, rosy apple by Walter ...

… only to find HALF a **FAT,** JUICY maggot inside.

(You can guess where the other

HALF was.)

How Walter

would

laugh!

And when his tutors finally left (as they always did), Walter would let

the dogs out to say goodbye.

Playing tricks made Walter happy – but that

jolly feeling never seemed to last very long.

Bored with playing fancy games and gadgets on his own, Walter

would sit in his HUGE bedroom gazing at the children of **Shoe**

Town as they laughed and skipped into school.

"WHY are *they* having MORE fun than me? And what's so good

about stupid SHOE SCHOOL anyway? It's not FAIR – I WANT

TO GO THERE TOO!" Walter had DEMANDED.

Reluctantly, Wendy had agreed, mostly because finding any new

tutors had become an impossible task.

(If you're starting to feel sorry for Walter, don't. He gets worse.)

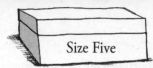

Size Five

Wendy ordered the Shoe School headmaster, Mr Moccasin, to come to WOW footquarters. She sat Mr Moccasin in the smallest, squeakiest and MOST uncomfortable chair. (Wendy enjoyed making people feel awkward.) As Walter would be mixing with "ordinary" children, she insisted that her little darling be looked after.

Wendy told Mr Moccasin how clever Walter was and how LUCKY the school would be to have him. And that wasn't all.

"Walter needs a special desk," Wendy explained. **"Adjusted to exactly the right height and a chair to match. He has wonderful posture, like me, and I want to keep it that way. No one likes a sloucher."**

"Walter ALSO needs his own personal play space and should be excluded from anything he doesn't want to do. And for goodness' sake, put him in a class with children who have a brain. I don't want his finely-tuned mind turning to MUSH."

Mr Moccasin listened carefully and then replied, "Ms Wedge, of course we'll look after Walter and I'm sure he'll thoroughly enjoy being part of our wonderful school. But I can't promise everything you're asking. We do have OTHER children to think about as well."

(Which was brave of him.)

"Oh, REALLY?" Wendy said and raised an EYEBROW. She was not very impressed.

"Maybe THIS might help you FOCUS on MY son a little more?"

Wendy THUMPED a case stuffed full of money on to the table.

She pushed it over to Mr Moccasin and GLARED at him.

"I'm SURE your wonderful school could do with a few improvements here and there. New equipment? More lovely books? A new desk for YOU, perhaps?"

Mr Moccasin looked at the CASH and swallowed. "Well … I don't know what to say, that's very generous of you…" he managed to answer.

Wendy nodded. **"Isn't it? We can discuss renaming the school in my honour later."**

"Oh, I'm not sure about THAT…" Mr Moccasin began.

Wendy swiftly reached over and PULLED

the money back towards her.

"Think of the school trips, the heated swimming pool.

THINK of the CHILDREN, Mr Moccasin."

Wendy pulled a sad face.

Mr Moccasin was feeling the
pressure. Wendy was making it clear he
didn't really have a choice. WOW was a very
powerful company in **SHOE TOWN** and getting bigger all the time.

"Yes, that's a wonderful idea, Ms Wedge," Mr Moccasin quickly
corrected himself.

Wendy pushed the money back towards him and smiled. **"And
one more thing,"** she said. **"The constant noise of the children
running around? I can't BEAR it. I can HEAR everything from
WOW Footquarters."**

"But it's impossible to stop the children from moving or talking,
Ms Wedge," Mr Moccasin explained.

"NOTHING'S impossible," snapped Wendy. **"And I have the
PERFECT solution."**

"You do?" Mr Moccasin asked nervously.

"Yes. ALL the children will wear brand-new shoes of my own design," Wendy told Mr Moccasin. Her hand hovered over the CASH.

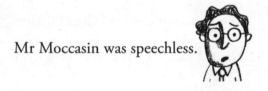

CLUMPY
shoes

"They're lovely and quiet and only *slightly* uncomfortable. So no more noise, a lot less running and hopefully we can CUT down on all that annoying laughter and FUN."

Mr Moccasin was speechless.

"Oh, and Walter will wear his OWN special WOWs."

(Of course he will.)

Mr Moccasin pulled himself together and thought about EVERYTHING she'd said. It wasn't EASY, but he told Wendy that Walter would be welcomed into the school just like any other child in **SHOE TOWN.**

"He's NOT like any other child, though – Walter is a GENIUS. He's a mini ME," Wendy corrected him. **"And you would do well to remember that."**

Mr Moccasin took a deep breath and told himself that Walter was only a small boy.

After all, how bad could he be?*

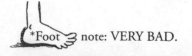
*Foot note: VERY BAD.

Size Six

Walter had arrived for his FIRST day of school clutching two bags STUFFED full of ...

TRICKS.

He'd got to work straight away – not with books or pens, but by making MISCHIEF.

Walter thought HE was HILARIOUS. (No one else did.)

Putting up with Walter just became part of the school day, as EVERYONE knew who his mother was. And after a

few weeks of playing the SAME tricks the SAME

I know it's fake, Walter...

kids, Walter had got bored.

He'd stomped around and insisted he be moved

to a different class. And, of course, Walter always got

what he wanted.

(No one was sorry to see him go.)

So today Walter was excited to have a FRESH bunch of kids to

 torment. He was looking forward to having some fun.

As soon as Bear saw the fancy new chair and plush

cushion next to his desk, he knew something

 was up. "Oh no," he sighed when he read the name

on the cushion.

But the sight of Walter striding towards him with his sharp black

fringe and menacing stare, looking like a small version of Wendy

(in trousers), was still alarming. Walter BOWED like he was royalty,

then said, "I'm here now – get used to it," before sitting down.

The school day began peacefully enough. Their teacher, Miss Mule, had set them a writing project and they were all working away quietly when Bear got up to fetch more paper. Walter took the opportunity to play his favourite trick. He was laughing before Bear even sat down.

Paaaarrrrrrpppppp! Ha! Ha! Ha!

"What's funny?" Bear asked him.

"Oh…" Bear rolled his eyes then handed the whoopee cushion back to Walter. "I think this belongs to you." Bear smiled weakly.

"Funny, right? And I've only just started," Walter bragged.

"I can tell," Bear said, and Walter laughed some more.

"Watch this – it always works a TREAT," he said and took out a FAKE spider (one of many he owned).

He THREW the spider into the middle of

the room where it landed on Freddie Flat's face.

"AGHHHHHHHHHH!"

Freddie screamed.

"What's going on?" Miss Mule demanded crossly.

Walter kept quiet and smirked.

Bear had the feeling that today wasn't going to be easy.*

*Foot note: THAT was putting it mildly.

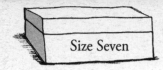

Size Seven

Ivor Foot was in trouble.

THIS is how much trouble

Ivor was in ...

An ENTIRE double-page spread

worth
of
trouble...

(Which is a lot.)

He'd come home to find a few white
feathers on the floor of Ruby and Bear's
bedroom.

Maybe they had a pillow fight? Ivor
thought. Or perhaps he had dropped them himself?
It was probably nothing. But Ivor decided to make sure the flying
shoes were safe – just in case.

He went into the kitchen and peeked out of the window to

check nobody was around, especially nosy
Mrs Court, then went to the table covered in
pictures of shoes. Ivor picked up a slightly wilting
vase of flowers and put them on the floor –

gently. The kids had picked them last week as a present for him.

"Right," he muttered, studying the table. "Come on, Ivor –

remember the combination."

The mosaic tabletop had been designed by Sally. And it HID

something SPECTACULAR.

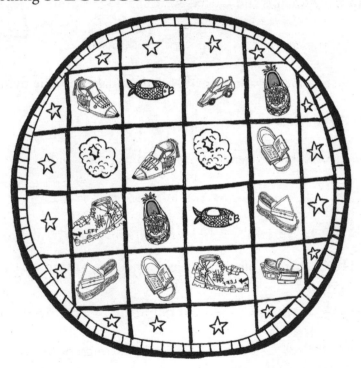

Pressing the shoe tiles down in the RIGHT order would open

up Ivor's secret workroom. He could NEVER remember what the

right order was, though.

Ivor was so busy trying to get the combination right that he didn't notice that the water in the vase had begun to RIPPLE and spill on the floor.

Or that the teacups and saucers were shaking on the shelves.

THIS was a clear sign that EITHER:

1. A HUGE herd of elephants was thundering towards the Foot house.

OR

2. Wendy Wedge was on her way – and she was in a VERY **BAD** mood.

(Take a WILD guess which one it was.)

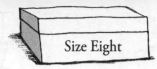

Size Eight

"GOT IT!" Ivor shouted. "Cloud shoes, drawing shoes, sandwich shoes, bird shoes, fish, cloud, cloud, fish, fish, book."

Nothing happened. "For goodness' SAKE, think..." he mumbled to himself.

"Cloud shoes, sandwich shoes, fish shoes, cloud, cloud, fish, fish, bird shoes, drawing shoes, book and THEN book. I always forget the second book."

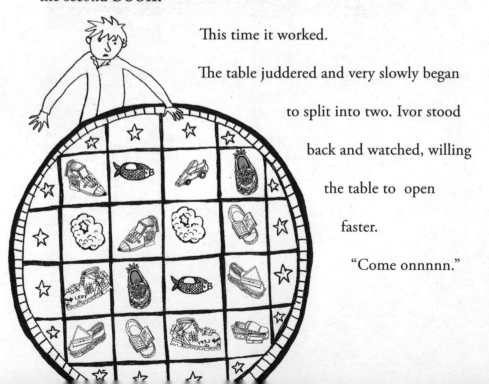

This time it worked.

The table juddered and very slowly began to split into two. Ivor stood back and watched, willing the table to open faster.

"Come onnnnn."

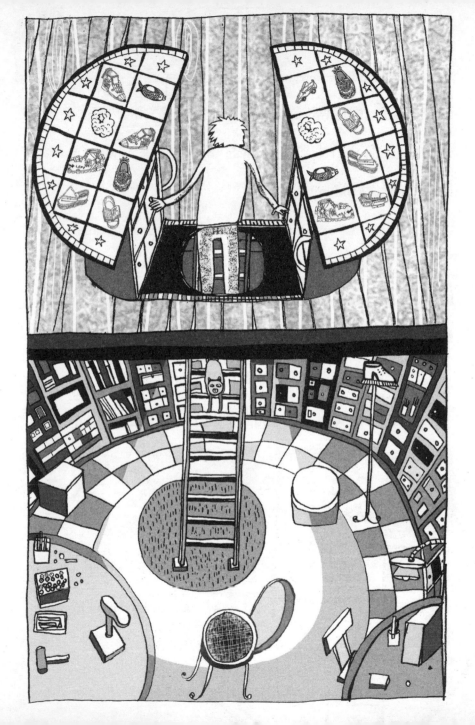

The shelves inside were stuffed full of tiny

boxes filled with buttons, bolts, beads, flowers, wires, ribbons, metal

springs, miniature trees, toy animals and all kinds of weird and

wonderful bits and bobs.

 Ivor ran his hand up and down a shelf, then stopped

at a plain-looking wooden shoebox with a lock on

the side.

"That's a good sign – it's here."

Ivor breathed a sigh of relief as he looked round for the key.

Holding the box with one hand, the lid DROPPED off and two

plain-looking shoes fell on to the floor.

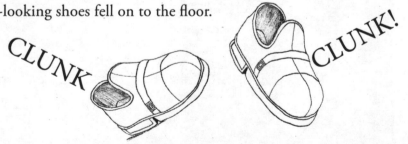

"Uh-oh… That's NOT a good sign," Ivor said to himself,

realizing the shoebox was already UNLOCKED.

He picked up the shoes and checked them over.

They seemed to be fine apart from a splash of red

paint on one side. Ivor touched the paint with his

finger; it was still wet.

WHERE had the paint come from?

There wasn't time to think, as in the kitchen the water from the

vase was already sloshing over the sides. And the teacups and saucers

were RATTLING together like crazy.

Ivor looked up.

"I need to get this table shut

RIGHT NOW!"

He had to act FAST.

Ivor put the shoes away and rushed back up the ladder to close

everything up.

"Stay calm and everything will be just fine*. You can DO this.

There's no need to panic," Ivor muttered to himself.

*Foot note: Everything was not going to be fine...

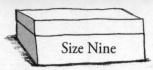

Size Nine

Thud...
Thud... Thud...
THUD!

The footsteps were heading towards Ivor's house, and he could

hear dogs BARKING too. The colour DRAINED from Ivor's face

as he tried once again to press the tiles down in the RIGHT order.

"Come on. Please WORK!" he muttered, now definitely panicking.

"Think, THINK!"

The glasses on the shelves clunked together and the ground began

to SHAKE. ALL his shoemaking secrets WERE THERE

for anyone to SEE!

"Deep breaths…"

Ivor KEPT pressing

the tiles, but the table

still wasn't closing.

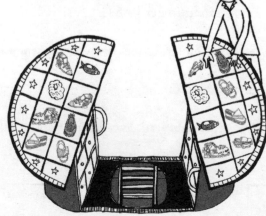

THUD THUD
THUD!

The footsteps came to a HALT right OUTSIDE Ivor's front door …

and then everything went quiet. (But not for long.)

The door started to RATTLE and then there was a LOUD

KNOCK

KNOCK

KNOCK

KNOCKING.

Ivor could hear the dogs **GROWLING** too.

He shouted as loudly and calmly as he could,

"I'm on my way! Won't be long!"

KNOCK! KNOCK! KNOCK! KNOCK!

"Be with you in a minute!"

The whole front door shuddered as someone started SHAKING

the handle.

"HOLD ON, I'll be RIGHT WITH YOU!"

Ivor shouted, frantically stabbing the squares with his finger.

"Yes, that's it!"

The table began to MOVE and the sides drew together slowly.

CLICK. AT LAST! The table looked like a table again.

"Calm down ... deep breaths," Ivor told himself,

as he took one last look around.

"I'm HERE!" he called, rushing to the door.

"I'm on my way! Here I come! I AM—"

Just as a

MASSIVE

METAL

WEDGE

SHOE

kicked open the door!

CLONK!

The unmistakable silhouette of Wendy Wedge stood in the doorway. With her huge shoulder pads and thick belt pulled in tight at the waist, Wendy cast a triangular shadow all the way into the house. She paused for effect (and also all that knocking had made her out of breath).

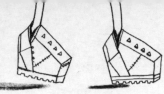

Her dogs, Left and Right, prowled and growled around her uncomfortable-looking metal wedges. Wendy STOMPED in, making everything around her shake even more.

"Wendy! What a lovely surprise. I had no idea you were coming!" Ivor said, wiping his forehead.

"What took you so long? I had to let myself in," she said, peering round suspiciously.

"I noticed. Sorry for the delay, I was—"

"WHAT were you doing?" Wendy demanded to know.

"I was … washing…"

Wendy interrupted him again. **"Washing?"**

Ivor's mind went blank, so he said the first thing that popped into his head.

"Yes – a beetroot."

"A beetroot?" she repeated.

"I … like very … clean vegetables," he found himself telling her.

Wendy just stared at him, unblinkingly, like a snake about to attack.

"What can I do for you, Ms Wedge? Is everything OK?" Ivor said, trying to sound relaxed.

"NO, Ivor, everything is NOT OK," Wendy replied.

She thumped past him into the kitchen.

Clump. Clump. Clump. Clump.

Wendy walked up and down, until one of the dogs got in her way and she stumbled.

"You two, wait over there and keep watch," Wendy ordered Left and Right sternly.

Ivor walked past them, and they growled. "Nice doggies," he whispered.

Ivor could usually tell what mood Wendy was in from the shoes she was wearing. Today she was VERY:

CROSS, CRANKY and ANGRY.

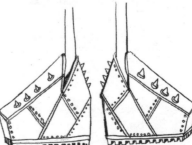

(But not necessarily in that order.)

Wendy caught Ivor staring at her feet.

 "Looking at something, Ivor?"

"Just admiring your shoes, Ms Wedge. You do have a

wonderful collection."

"That's true. I have the finest WEDGES in the world." Wendy

smiled, but not in a good way.

"Although, Ivor, there is ONE pair

of SHOES that Iwould very much like to ADD to my collection.

Any idea what they could be?" Wendy narrowed her eyes until

they disappeared into her face like straight little lines.

"Oh, that's a tough one," Ivor said, smiling cheerily, which was a

mistake. "I'd say lovely, soft, comfy shoes? Something like a slip—"

Wendy leaned into Ivor's face.

Furious face

"Is that your idea of a JOKE, Ivor? Slip—

I can't even SAY the word.*

THOSE SHOES
are ILLEGAL."

She thumped her foot down so hard, the dogs lifted off

the ground.

"Are they really, Ms Wedge?" Ivor said.

This was NEWS to him.

*Foot note: The word is 'slippers', in case you were wondering.

Wendy turned her back on Ivor, then STOMPED towards the kitchen. She paused at the table and began drumming her fingers on the shoe tiles.

"NO, Ivor. The ONE pair of shoes that I don't have in my collection begins with an F."

Ivor was starting to sweat.

"Shoes beginning with F? LET me guess: Flippers? Flip-flops? FURRY shoes?"

"FLYING SHOES, IVOR! I don't yet have a pair of FLYING SHOES. But somebody ELSE in Wedge Town DOES!"

Wendy fixed him with a *GLARE.*

Ivor tried to look shocked. "REALLY? Surely a pair of

shoes that can fly is IMPOSSIBLE?"

"Oh, they exist, Ivor, and I'm GOING to find

out WHO has them, even if I have to search every

house in Wedge Town."

"Don't you mean **SHOE TOWN,** Ms Wedge?" Ivor asked.

"NOT any more. I think Wedge Town has a certain ring to it,

don't you agree?"

(Ivor didn't.)

"We've all tried to make flying shoes for you many times, Ms

Wedge," he reminded her. "And no one has succeeded."

"WELL, SOMEONE HAS SUCCEEDED! And is trying to

keep them a secret," she snarled. **"AND I NEED THOSE**

FLYING SHOES TO WIN THE GOLDEN SHOE

AWARD!"

Wendy pointed an accusing finger at Ivor.

"YOU used to make shoes with gadgets, didn't you? In that little shop you used to run."

"Not really – they were just plain old boring shoes … nothing like the AMAZING ones we – I mean, YOU – create at World of Wedge," Ivor added quickly.

But Wendy wasn't convinced.

"Hmmmmmm." Wendy began to look around his kitchen. She stopped to pick up a picture frame.

"Oh, look," she said. **"Your lovely wife. Dear Sally Sandal. How we miss her. Such a terrible tragedy – to die from a teeny weeny little snake bite."**

Ivor took the picture from Wendy and carefully put it back.

"Yes," he said quietly. "We all miss her very much."

"It's hard bringing up children on your own," Wendy said. **"I know that only too well. And very difficult keeping them out of trouble. YOUR TWO, for instance. Did you know they were sent home from school EARLY today?"**

"No, I didn't know that," Ivor said.

Wendy's voice grew softer and more menacing.

"Walter told me ALL about it. They had EXTRA gadgets in their school WOW shoes. Which is SERIOUSLY breaking the RULES."

Ivor gulped. "You know what kids are like, they were probably just showing off. I'll talk to them later, Ms Wedge."

"NO, I'll talk to them RIGHT NOW. And I think I'll ask them about the FLYING shoes too. It's quite the coincidence, isn't it?"

"They won't know anything about the flying shoes and neither do I." Ivor stood up and tried to sound calm. "Maybe whoever saw them made a mistake?"

"Are you calling my son a LIAR?" Wendy asked.

"No, no, absolutely not, Ms Wedge."

"Because my Walter NEVER lies. He said a person dropped RED PAINT all over him and then flew OFF!"

"Really? That's terrible. Is Walter OK?" Ivor asked her.

She shrugged. **"He's still slightly red and wasn't happy about having a bath. But the POINT IS, Ivor…"**

Wendy THUMPED the mosaic table with her fist.

She hit it SO hard a crack appeared in the middle.

Ivor held his breath.

"SOMEONE in
WEDGE TOWN ..."

THUMP

"HAS GOT FLYING SHOES!"

THUMP

"AND I MUST HAVE

THEM!

THUMP

"I *HAVE* TO WIN ..."

THUMP

"'THE

GOLDEN ..."'

THUMP

"'SHOE

AWARD."'

THUMP!

On the LAST **thump,** the table creaked. And then, to Ivor's

horror, it started opening ever so slightly.

"NO!" Ivor shouted.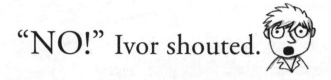

"What do you mean, NO?" Wendy said.

 She looked confused. "No" wasn't a word she

heard very often.

"Sorry, I just meant ... the table's delicate,

Ms Wedge. You don't want to hurt your hand if a tile breaks."

Wendy stared at Ivor.

"Do you remember signing a contract, Ivor?"

(How could he forget?)

"I do, Ms Wedge. It was very long with a lot of teeny tiny writing on it that was extremely hard to read."

"Well, I can tell you what it said. ALL the shoes you have ever made in your whole entire LIFE now belong to World of Wedge – that's me. And not 'some shoes', Ivor. ALL OF THEM."

Ivor kept quiet.

"And I would HATE for you to lose your job and everything you own. After all, who would look after your children?" Wendy began to trace a long, pointy finger over the painted shoes tiles again, tapping them in a way which made Ivor nervous. He could see the gap all her THUMPING had opened up.

The contract was MASSIVE with a LOT of conditions written in tiny teeny writing.

SIGN HERE
Ivor Foot

"I DESERVE to win **THE GOLDEN SHOE AWARD,**

don't you think? This year I WILL win it. And DO YOU know

HOW that's going to happen, IVOR?"

"You've bribed all the judges?" Ivor guessed.

"NO – BY ENTERING WITH FLYING SHOES!" Wendy shouted and stamped

her foot again. A small HATCH opened from the back

of her wedge and a metal claw SPRUNG out.

"**Not now!**" Wendy snapped and it popped back in.

Her STEELY eyes spotted the vase of flowers that Ivor had forgotten to put back on the table. **"Why are they on the floor?"** she asked.

"I was about to give them more water," he tried to explain.

Wendy picked them up and sniffed them.

"Ugh, revolting! Horrible dead weeds, THROW THEM OUT!"

"Ruby and Bear picked them for me. They're good kids, Wendy," Ivor told her.

"We'll see about that. Let's go and have that chat with them, shall we?" Wendy gave Ivor a terrifying smile.

"But, Ms Wedge…they're…"

Before he could say anything else, Wendy STOMPED OFF down the corridor.

It wasn't hard to find their room in such a small house.

Wendy stopped outside and SHOUTED...

"Ruby! Bear! It's your favourite Aunty Wendy here! I'm coming in to SAY HELLO!"

She glanced at Ivor.

"Why are they HIDING from me?"

"They're not, they're just..."

Wendy put on a horrible

sickly-sweet voice.

"I KNOW you're in THERE! READY OR NOT, HERE I COME!"

She SLID OPEN the door and went in.

"Ms Wedge, I was trying to tell you, they're ...

NOT ..." Ivor spluttered...

"... VERY WELL," he finished.

Ruby and Bear were standing there.

They were both covered in

BRIGHT
RED
SPOTS!

They looked up and WAVED in a slightly feeble way.

Wendy jumped back in horror. She hated any kind of illness

almost as much as she hated slippers.

"We're not feeling great, so we got into our pyjamas," Ruby said

in a really soft voice.

"We're listening to soothing music," Bear added hoarsely, pointing

to their headphones. Ivor was almost as surprised as Wendy to see them

at HOME with spots all over their faces. When had they got back?

"Oh no, you POOR things!" he said as Wendy continued to edge

away.

Ruby and Bear came closer.

"The spots just came UP. Do you want to see?" Ruby asked Wendy, who was already FREAKING out.

"STAY where you are – don't come NEAR me!" Wendy shouted, then turned to Ivor.

"Why didn't you tell me they were SICK, Ivor? Is it contagious? What have they got? WHY did you let me in the HOUSE if you knew they were covered in SPOTS?!"

"I didn't really have a choice," Ivor reminded her.

"KEEP THEM AWAY FROM ME."

Wendy looked down to see Shoo the cat

hiding behind her wedges. She bent down and

GRABBED her in a slightly ALARMING way, then held Shoo

up as a shield.

"I'm LEAVING NOW, BUT

I KNOW you're HIDING

SOMETHING. I WANT those

FLYING shoes!" Wendy told

them, still holding Shoo, who

hissed at her.

"You know something too, I bet," Wendy hissed back at Shoo.

"Nice fur. You'd make a lovely pair of kitten heels for me!" She

turned to Ivor. **"Just remember – I'll be WATCHING you, your**

spotty children and your CUTE little kitty."

"PUT Shoo DOWN! You're scaring her," Ruby said crossly.

"DON'T come any CLOSER." Wendy began to BACK away, still holding Shoo up for protection. The dogs ran over, BARKING like CRAZY as Shoo scrambled on to Wendy's shoulders to escape.

Wendy screamed, **"GET OFF ME!"** and Shoo obeyed, leaping off, sending Wendy wobbling backwards. She swung her arms round wildly, trying not to fall.

"WEDGES CONNECT! NOW!"

Wendy SHRIEKED and a large metal claw appeared from the

back of each WEDGE to keep her upright.

"Control yourselves, Left and Right!" Wendy shouted as she

wobbled out of the door.

Ivor quickly SLAMMED it shut behind her then took a BIG

deep BREATH IN.

"Did you see her face?" Ruby laughed.

"Her arms," Bear joined in, doing

an impression of Wendy falling.

Ivor double locked the door then

turned to the kids with a very SERIOUS face.

"Well, you've both made a quick recovery,"

he said suspiciously, rubbing one of the spots on

Bear's cheek with his finger. It smeared into a splodge.

"Red paint?" he asked.

"Maybe..." Ruby whispered.

"We had to do something, Dad! It was an emergency!" Bear

explained.

Ivor took out the feather he had found earlier and held it up in

front of them.

"This was in your room.

Any idea where it came from?"

he asked.

"A bird?" said Bear.

"OR a duck?" Ruby added.

"A duck IS a bird," Bear pointed out.

"You didn't say what kind of bird though – and ducks can be

white, so it could be from a duck. Or a pigeon…" Ruby said.

Ivor shook his head.

"Come on, you two – I think we need to have a little chat. After

you've washed off those fake spots," he said, looking at them sternly.

"You won't get cross, will you, Dad?" Ruby asked anxiously.

"Clean up first, then you can

tell me everything,*"

Shoo gets comfy

*Foot note: there was a LOT to tell.

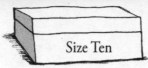
Size Ten

"You did WHAT?"

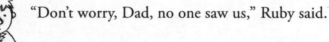

Ivor could hardly believe what he was hearing.

"Don't worry, Dad, no one saw us," Ruby said.

"We made sure of that," Bear added.

"Let me get this straight. You TOOK my flying shoes from my workshop. THEN you used them to FLY to the BRAND NEW Wedge Town sign and paint a heart over it?"

The kids nodded. "It looks so much nicer now, Dad. You should see it," Ruby told him.

KEY!

Ivor shook his head. "HOW did you even know where to FIND the shoes? I can't hide anything from you two, can I?"

"You could hide beetroot," said Ruby.

"We'd NEVER look for THAT."

"What's wrong with beetroot?" Dad sounded slightly confused.

"It tastes like soil!" Ruby pulled a face.

"How do YOU know what soil tastes like?"
Bear asked.

"I had some on a carrot once by accident, when I was little,"
Ruby told Bear. "It tastes kind of earthy, like beetroot. Yuck."

"Enough about BEETROOT! Shall we get back
to what you've both been up to behind my back?" Dad asked.

Ruby and Bear took deep breaths and started to tell Dad ALL
about Walter Wedge.

(Yes, HIM…)

"First of all, I found out that Walter Wedge had been moved to MY class at school," Bear said. "He was sitting right next to me."

"Oh dear…" Dad muttered.

"He pushed past us outside, like he was SO special," Ruby added.

 "Sounds like Walter Wedge. What happened next?" Dad wanted to know.

"He brought a BIG bag of FAKE spiders and bugs in to play tricks on me and everyone else. Walter put one on my seat and then chucked another at Fred Flat," Bear said.

"Did Walter get told off?" Dad asked.

"No way. Teachers aren't ALLOWED to tell Walter off," sighed Bear.

"But get this, Dad – Bear hid all Walter's tricks." Ruby sounded proud of her brother.

"Walter wasn't happy. But I was going to give them back eventually," Bear said.

"Nice one!" Ruby high-fived him.

"It put Walter in a VERY bad mood. He was super sulky and refused to take part in sports lessons. Walter's got a note from his mother that EXCUSES him from pretty much EVERYTHING he doesn't want to do," Bear said.

"*I'd* like one of *those*." Ruby smiled.

"Nice try, Ruby. Carry on, Bear,"

Dad said with a chuckle.

Uh-oh.

"So, Miss Mule suggested he go to the library if he wanted to.

Only he didn't. He waited until we were all in PE, then

SEARCHED the class for the fake bugs and

FOUND them in my desk. So he knew it was

me. Then he put them all in our shoes

and socks as a nice surprise."

Dad sighed. "Sounds like Walter."

"And that's when he must have spotted that

MY shoes had EXTRA gadgets inside – thanks

to you, Dad. They are great, by the way."

"Thanks, Bear," Dad said.

"He went straight to Mr Moccasin and showed him.

Then Mr Moccasin called me and Ruby into his office.

Walter was there smiling at us in a

'serves you right' kind of way."

"He told Mr Moccasin that his MOTHER was going to hear all

about my gadgets

and we should be given

a VERY BIG punishment.

"THEN he suggested LOADS of extra homework for a YEAR,

cleaning everyone's shoes, AND detentions too," Bear explained.

"Hey! I was the one who broke the shoe rules – not you two. I'm

going to call Mr Moccasin right now and explain," Dad interrupted.

"It's OK, Dad," Ruby said. "Mr Moccasin sent Walter off then told us

to go home early and to never wear the shoes again. And that was it! No

punishment!"

"Good for Mr Moccasin!" Dad said, pleased and relieved.

"We didn't want to get YOU in trouble, Dad. So I told him it was

US who changed the shoes," Bear said.

"Did he believe you?"

"He was impressed and told us to keep INVENTING – just not on our WOW school shoes," Bear said.

"Can we get to the part where you PINCHED my flying shoes now?" Dad asked.

"So, we were on our way home early and we popped in to see Bert in his shoe shop. He was busy painting protest signs," said Bear.

"Good old Bert," Dad told them. "His is the only shoe shop in town that's NOT owned by Wendy Wedge."

"Bert told us she wants to close down his shop," said Ruby.

"Ah."

"So we joined in and painted our own signs!"

Dad sighed. "Of course you did."

"Mine was the best. It said:

Don't BE SHOE-PID.
KEEP BERT'S SHOP OPEN!"

she added.

"He's got some fancy new

styles of shoes in his shop, Dad – you should see them," Bear said

excitedly. "And he knows lots of good stories about what **SHOE TOWN**

USED to be like, before Wendy Wedge took over. He showed us

photos of you and Mum when you were younger."

"With bad hair, Dad," Ruby told him.

"Hey – that was a good look back then,"

Ivor protested.

They both shook their heads. "No, Dad, it really wasn't."

"OK, so you went to Bert's, painted some protest signs and then

what did you do?"

"We left the shop and spotted Mr Creeper with a group of Wedge workers putting up the NEW Wedge Town sign," Ruby told Dad. "LIKE there aren't ENOUGH things NAMED after her already?"

"Why does Wendy get to put her NAME all over OUR town?" Bear wondered.

"Because SHE owns most of it," Dad explained sadly.

"Well, that's not fair! Anyway, we're both looking up at the SIGN and we decide **SHOE TOWN** is a MUCH better name than WEDGE TOWN. And that's when I had the BEST IDEA EVER!" said Ruby.

"We'd BORROW the flying shoes, FLY up to the sign and paint over it!" Bear said.

"HOW did you even know where my flying shoes were kept?" Dad wanted to know.

"You won't get cross?" Bear asked.

"I'll try not to."

"ONCE, I saw you open up the kitchen table. I was hiding behind the bookshelf," Bear told him.

"HEY, that's MY spot!" Ruby said.

"But how did you know the code? I can't even remember it most of the time," Dad asked.

"I have a good memory. I saw you do it once – and that was enough." Bear patted his head.

Dad began to look nervous.

"We were very careful with the shoes, Dad, I promise," Ruby assured him before continuing. "THEN, as we were leaving the house, Mrs Court suddenly appeared,

wondering why we weren't in school."

"She MUST have seen the shoes," Dad said.

"No, but she asked about the red paint we were carrying. I said it was for a school project, and we'd come home to collect it," Ruby told Dad.

"Good thinking, Ruby."

"I'm not sure she believed us. But then Shoo started purring all around her walking stick. That distracted her, so we sneaked off," Ruby explained.

"By the time we'd got to the sign, there was no one around. So I put on the shoes, and used the special-adjustment panel for different-sized feet. A VERY smart thing you added, Dad."

"I try my best," Dad said, blushing proudly.

"Then I gave Ruby a piggyback while she held on to the paint."

"And I said, nice and clearly, 'Shoes UP,'" Ruby added.

"We lifted off the ground, so I said it again – 'SHOES UP!' – and, really quickly, we got to the same height as the sign. It was AMAZING, Dad!"

"Then all Ruby had to do was paint a heart over the 'DGE' quickly, then she wrote 'SHOE', as I kept us steady," Bear continued.

"It says WE HEART **SHOE TOWN,** and looks loads better," Ruby said proudly.

"It was all going really well when the one person we DIDN'T want to see, Walter Wedge, started heading our way."

Dad looked a bit pale as Ruby picked up the story. "We quickly

FLEW behind a tree and hovered. Walter SPOTTED the sign – and

he wasn't HAPPY…"

"That's when we lost control of the shoes. They

SUDDENLY LURCHED to the left and then to the

right and the PAINT spilled out…" Bear paused.

"ON TO WALTER," Ruby said, trying not to smile.

"Of ALL the places it COULD have landed, it HAD to be ON

Wendy's SON," Dad said, knowing this was not good at all.

"It took a moment for it to sink in," Bear said.

"The paint?" Dad asked.

"No – where the paint had come from. Walter looked all confused."

"And all red too…" Ruby added.

"We tried to fly back to the house but the flying went WOBBLY.

We were ALL over the place!"

"HOW did no one see you?" Dad wondered.

"We were smart, Dad, we tried to fly low and Bear did a really good landing behind a TREE," said Ruby reassuringly.

"Then we rushed home to put the shoes BACK, but you were already in the house," Bear told him. "We had to figure out how to get past you."

"But HOW?" asked Dad. "I would have seen you."

"Oh, this bit's good," said Ruby.

"Ruby took a letter from our mailbox and posted it through Mrs Court's door," explained Bear.

"YES – and then she came round with it," Dad said. "THAT'S when you two sneaked in." Ruby and Bear nodded.

"Mrs Court's SO nosy, we knew she wouldn't just POST it back," Bear said. "And we knew she'd keep you chatting for ages."

"We climbed through the window while you chatted. Bear put the shoes back in the box and CLOSED up the table."

"The perfect crime," sighed Dad. "I suppose I should be impressed."

"Then after SHE left we heard all that THUMPING at the door," Bear carried on.

"WE knew that Walter would have blabbed. We had to think FAST! That's when we put the red paint on our faces. We knew that would do the trick. Wendy hates spots," Bear said, and high-fived Ruby.

Dad looked at them both. "Is that it – nothing more to add?"

Ruby and Bear shook their heads.

"What if you'd been caught? What if you had been hurt?" Dad asked.

"We're FINE AND the shoes are THE BEST! YOU should enter **THE GOLDEN SHOE AWARD,** Dad! You'd win it for sure!" Ruby exclaimed.

"You totally would!" Bear agreed.

"I can't," said Dad. "I signed a contract with World of Wedge. Every shoe I made, now and in the past, belongs to Wendy."

"But you didn't make the shoes," Bear said slowly. "Mum did. So you can enter them?"

Dad shook his head. "It's too risky. I can't prove that was Mum. Imagine if Wendy took them away? Your mum would hate that. She'd never forgive me."

"But, Dad, last night I heard you tell Shoo that Mum would be SO proud if you won **THE GOLDEN SHOE AWARD,"** Ruby reminded him.

"I was tired, Ruby. I'd be out of a job if that happened."

"You could work with Bert Brogue,
just like the old days. If you were
making flying shoes, everyone
would buy them, and he could keep
his shop open with all the NEW customers. You wouldn't need
Wendy Wedge."

Dad stood up. "It's not going to happen," he sighed. "Wendy
has plans to CLOSE DOWN Bert's shop. She'll find a way to do
it somehow. But she CAN'T take Sally's shoes as well. So do you
promise me – NO more flying shoe trips?"

Bear and Ruby mumbled a sort of yes.

"Pinky promise?" Dad asked, holding his finger out.

All three of them linked little fingers together and made a pact.

"Pinky promise."

135

Dad frowned. "Can anyone hear a weird buzzing noise?"

"Probably my stomach rumbling," Ruby suggested. "I'm really hungry. It's all that flying."

"Me too," said Bear. "What's for dinner?"

"Nothing with beetroot, I hope," Ruby told Bear, who pulled a face.

While the Foot family were busy making promises and talking about dinner, the tall shadowy figure of Mr Creeper was lurking around outside. And he had heard EVERYTHING.

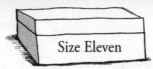

Size Eleven

Mr Creeper was Wendy's loyal and long-suffering assistant. Wendy trusted Mr Creeper, but it didn't stop her from being mean to him. (Like she was to most people.) So why did Mr Creeper stay working there?

Good question.

Wendy had always promised him a **MIGHTY BIG** promotion. "You'll be VERY important. Obviously not AS important as ME, but then who is?"

Mr Creeper kept hoping that Wendy would keep her promise. But it hadn't happened yet.

Wendy had STOMPED away from the Foots' house and with every step she became EVEN MORE convinced that Ivor Foot and his annoying children KNEW something about the flying shoes.

So she DEMANDED that Mr Creeper GO back to the **Shoebox Estate**. **"Those fiendish FOOTS are up to something, I know it. Find the EVIDENCE or, better still, find the flying shoes."**

"And if they're not there?" Mr Creeper had asked, which sent Wendy into a MASSIVE MELTDOWN.

"JUST GET ME THE FRYING SHOES!"

This confused Mr Creeper. "FRYING shoes?" he'd asked.

"Don't be RIDICULOUS.
I WANT those FLYING SHOES!"

Wendy's face had turned as RED as a strawberry.

Mr Creeper crept away as fast as he could.

He'd quickly thought of a plan. (In between thinking of biscuits...)

Mr Creeper headed straight to the WOW workshop (via a biscuit tin).

All the WEDGE creations for tomorrow's **GOLDEN SHOE**

AWARDS were kept there. (The workshop, not the biscuit tin.)

He'd just borrow the impressive CAMERA WEDGES that Ivor Foot had been working on. Did he feel guilty about PINCHING Ivor's shoes?

No, he did not.

"This is a SHOEmergency,*" Mr Creeper said to himself, with a mouth full of custard cream.

*Foot note: An emergency – but for shoes.

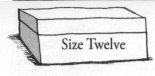 

Size Twelve

$\mathbf{M}$r Creeper changed out of his own footwear (which was a bit

grim), lifted the temperature-controlled glass dome off Ivor's camera

wedges and put them on. Then he activated the AUTOMATIC

shoe adjuster so the wedges would fit his own feet perfectly.

(For a tall man, Mr Creeper had very tiny toes.)

Next he clipped the control panel on to his wrist and said,

"TURN. WEDGES. ON."

Nothing happened.

He repeated it again and again in

different tones of voice, but none of them worked.

"So annoying…" he mumbled. Then he spotted what looked

like an instruction

booklet, open to the

page that said...

WARNING:
USE THE
SUPER PUSH
CONTROL
WITH . . .

**EXTREME
CAUTION**

"Noted…"

Mr Creeper said, logging it in his memory. He flicked through the

booklet until he found a page that said

TECHNICAL PROBLEMS.

"This is what I need," he muttered.

"If the voice control isn't responding, try turning it OFF and

then ON again."

Which seemed to do the trick.

The WEDGES sprung into life.

Mr Creeper glanced at his reflection

in the window. "Not bad…" He nodded

approval to himself.

"Not bad at all."

Now all set with the camera wedges on his feet, he made his way back to the Foots' house. He strode past the two guards on the WOW door, and a quick wave of his pass lifted the barrier up.

"You haven't seen me," Mr Creeper hissed at them. "And you definitely haven't seen me wearing these WEDGES."

Mr Creeper crept down to the **Shoebox Estate,** glancing round to make sure no one was watching, before darting behind a particularly WIDE TREE right outside the Foots' house.

He then tapped the screen on his wrist, and using the voice control, whispered to "RAISE wedges UP" for a better view.

Mr Creeper could see the family were sitting round the table talking.

"Perfect." He smiled menacingly. Then he stretched out his RIGHT foot and whispered, "Release camera."

From a hatch in his heel, a long metal arm slowly uncurled down from his shoe. It slithered along the ground, and then crept up the side of the house until it was pointed directly at the Foots' window.

Mr Creeper checked the screen on his wrist to get a good clear picture.

"Focus and record."

The sound was a bit muffled at first, but he could distinctly make

out some kind of … purrrring, just before the whole screen went

DARK.

"Camera," he whispered urgently. "Left, down, focus. FOCUS."

Suddenly, TWO BRIGHT EYES ZOOMED into view and were

STARING right at him.

"Out of the way – OI! Stupid CAT!" He tried moving the

camera but all he could see was its TAIL swishing backwards and

forwards.

Finally, Mr Creeper managed to get high enough so the cat couldn't block his view, just in time to HEAR Ivor say TWO VERY IMPORTANT WORDS:

"FLYING SHOES."

Mr Creeper listened and listened and smiled an evil smile.

"YES! Thank you, Ivor Foot. I heard you nice and clearly – and so will everyone else now." HE HAD EVIDENCE! Mr Creeper would WAFT Ivor's contract around to remind him what he'd agreed, the **Shoe Police** could be his back-up and look stern, and Wendy could take what was rightfully hers: the flying shoes.

It was time to get back. Wendy would be thrilled and CONGRATULATE him – and MAYBE give him that long-awaited promotion? He deserved it.

Mr Creeper was imagining himself sitting in a new office, with NEW shoes and his feet on the desk when *PING!*

SOMETHING stung him on the NECK.

"Ow!" It felt like a wasp sting.

There was another *PING* that HIT something above his HEAD.

"I hate wasps," he said, looking around. It was time to get out of here. Mr Creeper whispered into his wrist control, "Bring camera back."

It slid back down the wall and was shrinking towards him when it STOPPED with a jolt. The camera was caught on something.

"What now?" repeated Mr Creeper. "Camera back. NOT YOU again," he sighed when he saw what it was.

Shoo had pounced on the camera like it was a MOUSE.

"Water jet ON," Mr Creeper said and watched Shoo get

soaked, then JUMP up and let go.

"Good. Now bring camera back!"

It slid across the ground, back inside his wedge heel with a

satisfying click.

"Phew," he muttered as something began to *BUZZ* around

his head. It was another WASP. He tilted his foot upright to check

it was all closed up. It was time to leave.

"Get lost!" he murmured under his breath and

SWIPED at it with his hand.

Then *PING!*

He was stung on the other side of his neck.

Mr Creeper smacked his skin to flatten whatever

was underneath. *PING!*

It got him on his arm next.

PING! Then his CHEEK.

PING! He slapped his own

face to get rid of the wasp, but

it landed on his wrist control.

After shaking it a few times, Mr Creeper

got CROSS and BASHED the controls

several times with his other hand. "Take

THAT!" he hissed, before accidentally

HITTING the **SUPER
PUSH-UP
CONTROL
function.**

The wedges made a weird noise that didn't sound good.

"Oh, no," he whispered, but it was too late.

They tipped him right BACK on maximum POWER,

then

SHOT

him UP

in the

air

like

a

cork

from

a

bottle.

Mr Creeper reached out for the nearest branch and hung on for as long as he could (which wasn't long).

He looked up and saw a wasp nest was RIGHT NEXT TO HIS HANDS! "Uh-oh!" He let go and dropped to the ground with a THUD. "Stupid wasps," Mr Creeper grumbled and dusted himself off. Checking the CAMERA wedges were still working, he put them back on and vowed NEVER to press that button again.

"Lucky escape. Now back to tell Wendy the GOOD news," he said ... just as the wasp nest CRASHED DOWN by his feet and the wasps ANGRILY SWARMED OUT all over him.

Mr Creeper RAN as fast as he could while trying to shake the WASPS off. He LEAPED over the WOW barrier like a hurdler. The guards screamed, "STOP! INTRUDER!"

and let the dogs loose.

"It's ME! It's ME!" Mr Creeper shouted.

He stumbled into the W-shaped fountain, taking cover under the water spray to SAVE himself, forgetting all about the high-tech camera wedges he still had on his feet.

(No, the shoes were not waterproof.)

Mr Creeper stayed there until the wasps left and the guards called off the dogs.

Things could only get better for Mr Creeper.*

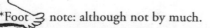
*Foot note: although not by much.

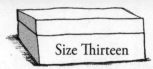

It was early morning when Walter came to see Wendy, who was

sitting at her dressing table and putting on her face.

"Walter, my little WEDGE, are you OK?

You look a tiny bit … PINK? It's not a rash, is it?"

Wendy asked, putting on her fake eyelashes and

leaning away (just in case it was catching).

"No!" Walter snapped. "It's still the RED PAINT! I can't get it off.

I've had TWO baths and I HATE washing! You have to find out who

did this to me, Mother."

"Poor Walty, I PROMISE we'll find the culprits. I already

have my suspicions," Wendy assured him.

"GOOD, because they need to be punished. I'll put itching

powder in their socks and set the DOGS on them!" Walter hissed,

keen for revenge.

"Of course you will. Those weasels RUINED my Wedge Town

sign too," Wendy told him.

Wendy held up the EYEBROW chart next to her face.

What SHAPE for today?

CROSS?

SURPRISED?

FIERCE?

She settled on

FIERCE and began to draw them on as Walter watched.

"TODAY is VERY important, Walter," she explained. **"My WEDGE workers are presenting their shoe creations to me, and they'd better be good. I HAVE to win THE GOLDEN SHOE AWARD this year. NO one is EVER going to laugh at me again."** She stopped, noticing that Walter was looking confused.

"What's wrong? Too fierce?" Wendy asked.

"Too WONKY. A bit like a wobbly worm, Mother,"

Walter pointed out.

(Not the look Wendy was going for.)

She wiped them off and redrew them swiftly.

"What about MY face?" Walter asked, feeling fed up.

"You look GORGEOUS – just like me, only pinker and with less fabulous eyebrows. The paint will come off … eventually," Wendy reassured him.

"Well, I'm not having another bath – EVER!" Walter said crossly.

Wendy ignored his comment and looked round impatiently for Mr Creeper.

"Where is that man? He SHOULD be here RIGHT now with important NEWS for me. What's taking him so long?"

Wendy was getting irritated. She picked up the phone. **"FIND Mr Creeper and tell him to get a MOVE on,"** she barked at a minion. As she slammed down the phone, there was a KNOCK at the door.

"About TIME!" Wendy shouted as the door began to slowly open.

In came a limping, shuffling figure covered in plasters and bandages and making a terrible sound.

Wendy looked alarmed (her eyebrows made her look even more so) as the person got closer. "MOTHER, who's that?" Walter shouted.

"Stay back!" Wendy yelled at the figure. But it kept shuffling closer, gradually taking off bandages and plasters to speak. **"ONE step nearer and I'm calling the DOGS! LEFT and RIGHT – SEIZE them!"** Wendy screamed. But the person kept coming.

So Wendy protected herself the ONLY way she knew how.

By **SHOVING** Walter in front of her.

"It's only meeeeee…" the intruder managed to

 *Mother!* say before the dogs ran in

SNARLING and GRABBED a leg

EACH in their mouths.

"AGGGHH! Noooooh … it's ME!

Mr Creeper!" he SQUEALED.

"For goodness' sake, Mr Creeper, WHAT

ARE you playing at?" Wendy asked furiously as she finally

recognized him. **"Put him down."**

Reluctantly, Left and Right let go of his legs.

"You look a MESS! And, much more importantly, DO you

HAVE MY flying shoes?"

"I've GOT the proof here that Ivor Foot DOES have them." Mr

Creeper held up the camera wedges, now battered and covered in

pondweed.

"WHAT on EARTH happened?" Wendy asked.

"I got really badly stung by…"

Mr Creeper started to say.

"NO. I'm not interested in YOU."

(Wendy didn't do sympathy.)

"Oh, of course you're not. You were right, Ms Wedge. Ivor's broken his contract. He made FLYING shoes and kept them hidden from you. AND I've got his confession on record."

If Mr Creeper was expecting to be congratulated by Wendy, it didn't happen.

"ARE YOU an IDIOT?" Wendy asked, seething with anger.

"I don't want to see PICTURES, I want the REAL DEAL."

"Absolutely. WHAT was I thinking? I'll call the SHOE POLICE RIGHT NOW to search the house," Mr Creeper said quickly, frantically trying to make things better.

By this time Walter had got bored and wandered off to peer out of the BIG, wedge-shaped window.

"Look, Mother! It's the FOOTS! Let's send the dogs to get them NOW!" he shouted, pointing at Ivor, Ruby and Bear, who were on their way to school.

Wendy glanced down. **"Well spotted, Walter. Look at them skipping away, not a care in the world. The dogs can wait: I have other plans. Be patient, Walter. That FOUL FOOT FAMILY have been lying to me for all this time,"** she hissed. **"Ivor won't be going ANYWHERE until I get MY shoes. And as for his AWFUL children, I'll deal with them later."**

"WITH ITCHING POWDER!" Walter screeched. He picked up the trick he'd been saving for a special occasion.

GENIUS

"You are SO clever, Walter. Isn't he, Mr Creeper?"

Mr Creeper nodded as if his life depended on it.*

"Ivor will be looking for his camera wedges. I think it's time for some FUN," Wendy added, rubbing her hands together at the thought of what was to come.

"In the meantime, YOU GET me those flying shoes, Mr Creeper. NOTHING should be left to chance. I don't want EXCUSES – WHATEVER it takes, JUST DO IT!" Wendy told him, then awkwardly WINKED. Which Mr Creeper mistook for a TWITCH.

"DO YOU UNDERSTAND?" she asked him again.

Mr Creeper tried to nod back, but his neck was too painful. And thanks to Walter, he was starting to ITCH in places he shouldn't.

He was NOT having a good day.

*Foot note: it did.

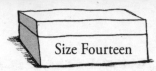

Size Fourteen

Ivor dropped the kids off at school and hurried his way through the gates of World of Wedge. It was the BIG SHOE presentation day, and everyone would be trying to IMPRESS Wendy by demonstrating their own Wedge shoe creations.

Ivor was hoping that his camera shoes would impress Wendy so much she'd forget about the flying shoes. They might even win **THE GOLDEN SHOE AWARD.** (It was a long shot, but Ivor could only do his best.) He tried to RELAX as he joined his co-workers in the locker room.

"Morning, Parminda Platform. Big day ahead."

"Tell me about it." She smiled nervously.

"How's things, Harry Heel?

Nice beard trim, by the way."

Ivor put on his WOW white coat.

"All set for **THE GOLDEN SHOE AWARD** presentation, Ivor?" Pauline Plimsoll asked.

"As ready as I'll ever be," Ivor sighed.

"I've heard Wendy's in a right mood," Pauline said, lowering her voice. "We could be in for a toe-curling day if she's not happy. Remember last time? She forced us to work all night long on HER LIFT-OFF WOODEN wedges, when we all KNEW they were too heavy to fly."

Ivor shrugged. "Wendy doesn't listen. She's obsessed with winning **THE GOLDEN SHOE AWARD.** It wasn't our fault they never took off."

"Shhh, she might hear you," Pauline said and scanned her pass to get into the workshops. BEEP.

Next, Ivor scanned his. It didn't BEEP.

He tried again. And again. He turned to the other workers and apologized.

"Sorry, I'm not sure what's wrong."

Then a face appeared on the screen.

It was their supervisor **Lottie Loafer.**

"Morning, Lottie. Why can't I get in? Is there a problem?" Ivor asked.

"Ms Wedge wants you to head straight to her office for the presentations today, Ivor. And Ms Wedge says she'd BETTER be impressed. Or else."

"IMPRESSED is my middle name," Ivor said.

"Is it?"

"No, Lottie. I just make jokes when I'm nervous," he explained.

"You need better jokes," Lottie said, then disappeared off the screen.

Ivor did not have a good feeling about today.

BEEP!
BEEP!

Mr Creeper was waiting for him outside Wendy's office. He was moving oddly and still had plasters on his face. He motioned for Ivor to wait.

"What happened to you?" Ivor asked.

"Wasp nest," Mr Creeper said very matter-of-factly, which put Ivor on edge.

"Shouldn't I be getting my WEDGES ready to present like everyone else?" Ivor asked cautiously. But Mr Creeper just stared ahead and ignored him.

"So, what DO I get to present to Ms Wedge then?" Ivor tried once more.

Mr Creeper pointed to Wendy's office door. "Your WEDGES are already in there," he snapped and scratched his foot.

"Well, that's all right then." Ivor smiled at him.

Mr Creeper didn't smile back.

"SssssssssHHHHHHhhhhhhhhhhhhhhh."

Ivor was joined by Betty Boot, who sat down next to him and

raised an eyebrow in a "what's going on?" kind of way. "Where are

YOUR camera wedges?" she whispered.

Ivor shrugged his shoulders.

"In there already, apparently,"

he said quietly.

The rest of the WOW team arrived. They'd finished cleaning,

polishing and adjusting their SHOWCASE wedges and now all that

was left was the PRESENTATION to Wendy. Whose wedges would

impress her the most?

Mr Creeper slid the door open. "You can go in now," he told

them.

"What happened to you?" Harry Heel asked.

"Nothing, what do you mean? I'm completely fine," Mr Creeper told him.

"You don't look fine," Betty pointed out.

They all wheeled in the glass domes covering their various shoe creations, apart from Ivor. He still couldn't see his camera wedges. *What is Wendy up to?* he wondered.

The room went dark and purple lights began to flash on and off from behind huge glass sliding doors. The team watched as Wendy and Walter appeared in silhouette. Wendy loved a BUILD UP and never missed an opportunity to make an entrance.

They HELD their pose and waited for the music to begin.

None of this was helping Ivor feel less nervous. Betty whispered to him, "Purple's a good colour."

"If you're a grape," he replied, and they both tried not to laugh.

"Shouldn't Walter be in shoe school?" Betty wondered.

"He's being trained up for great things," Ivor told her.

"Or GRAPE things…" Betty laughed again.

The dogs growled at them and Mr Creeper glared in their direction, so they stopped talking.

The doors began to slide open as the music started …

… only it wasn't the music she was expecting.

"WHAT IS THIS, CIRCUS MUSIC? I'm NOT a CLOWN!"

Wendy bellowed.

"Sorry, sorry – I don't know what happened…" a voice

behind the glass door said quickly and replaced the cheerful

comedy TUNE with some **STRIDENT, BOLD**

marching music.

Wendy STOMPED purposefully into the room and sat down in

the dark velvet chair placed behind her slick-looking desk. Walter

had been told to wait until he was called, and he wasn't looking

very happy.

Wendy was still in silhouette and said, "You can all clap now…"

There was polite applause, as no one really wanted to be there.

"Good morning. How are we all?" Wendy asked briskly.

Phillip Flop began to answer. "We're all feeling—"

Wendy held up her hand and stopped him. **"No need to reply, I'm not really interested. Although I HOPE it will be a good morning for ME. I'm on the wEDGE of my seat, WAITING to be impressed today. My wonderful son, Walter, will be joining us for the judging. You may ALL clap for Walter."**

Walter STRODE in looking smug (although still slightly pink from the paint.) He sat down next to Wendy and almost disappeared from sight.

"Someone get Walter a  **cushion, or maybe two…"** Wendy called out and glanced down at Walter. **"Make that three cushions."** The cushions appeared quickly and Walter plonked them on his chair.

"Where were we…?" Wendy asked now that the problem was FIXED.

"As you all know, **THE GOLDEN SHOE AWARDS** are

tomorrow and I intend to win. NOT for best special effects

shoes or for the best shoe you can EAT. None of that nonsense,

not this time. It's the top prize I want. NOW LET'S SEE

WHICH OF YOU has made me the

WINNING WEDGES."

She pointed to Betty. **"You first..."**

Betty Boot pushed her wedges towards Wendy and lifted up the

glass dome to give her a closer look. Wendy tapped her nails on the

desk. **"They look dull. What do**

they do?" she asked, frowning.

"They make music, Ms Wedge.

Everyone needs music in their lives,"

Betty told her.

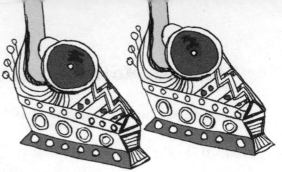

"Not everyone."

Wendy narrowed her eyes as she watched Betty take off her white coat and put the wedges on.

"Come on, Betty Boot, get a move on," Wendy bellowed at her impatiently.

"Yes, hurry UP," Walter added.

Betty could feel Wendy's stony gaze on her. It was making her fingers wobble. She tried to keep calm and checked the wedges were sitting securely on her feet.

Each one had lots of different-coloured buttons, dials, lights, switches and lightning bolts, as well as TWO big speakers on the front.

Betty took a moment to breathe, and then began to tap one foot. The sound of tapping kept going after she'd stopped. Then she clapped her hands and tapped her other foot. The claps and taps were recorded and repeated to build up a rhythm.

"Get on with it, will you?" Wendy hissed.

Betty tapped her feet once more, and Wendy's VOICE started to come OUT of the shoe speakers.

"Get on with it, will you...?

Get, get, get on with it, will you?

You, you,

get on with it,

will you...?"

Wendy frowned and folded her arms, waiting to be impressed.

"Then," said Betty, "you can put it all together like THIS!"

The wedges began to play music, the lights flashing in time to the beat. Small wheels popped out under the wedges and Betty began to SPIN round in a circle.

She danced spectacularly, without any effort at all, zooming

forwards, backwards, and finishing with an amazing super-speedy spin.

Betty STOPPED and threw her arms in the air. "Tah-dah! It's all in the

WEDGES, no dancing skills required. You record the music and the

dance feature KICKS in, so anyone can DANCE in these wedges."

Ivor and the other Wedge workers CLAPPED enthusiastically.

Wendy rested her hand under her chin and yawned. **"I've seen enough. Walter, what do you think?"** she asked. Walter wrinkled his nose up.

"Booooooooorrring," he said.

"EXACTLY. WHERE was the WOW-factor, Betty? I've seen dancing shoes before. Do you think all the shoemakers of Sneakerville or Shoecastle will be quaking in their boots? I don't think so. NEXT!" Wendy shouted.

Betty sat down again, slightly out of breath from the dancing.

"Well, I thought they were great," Ivor whispered.

"Thanks, but what was I thinking, making them FUN? For Wendy?" Betty whispered back.

Phillip Flop and Parminda Platform were up next. They both stepped forwards.

Wendy rolled her eyes. **"Oh no, it's YOU two..."** Which didn't help their confidence.

"Ms Wedge. In a world with many stresses and strains, we're all looking for something to CALM our nerves..."

"You're getting on MY nerves already. Hurry up..." Wendy snapped.

Phillip laughed nervously.

"Ms Wedge, Parminda Platform and I will be demonstrating the magical, mind-healing POWER of WEDGE-I-TATION!" He gulped, then added, "Like … meditation, but with wedges."

"SERIOUSLY?" Wendy rolled her eyes some more. There was a box in front of them with gold fabric draped over it. Parminda stepped onto it with bare feet. She took a deep breath and closed her eyes.

"This had better be good," Walter murmured.

The thick gold fabric began to wrap itself around each foot, moulding to Parminda's toes and coming together at each ankle. Parminda kept her eyes closed and her head up, HOPING it was all going to plan.

"They don't look very … WEDGE-like," Wendy noted.

"Just wait," Phillip said. Parminda reached down and touched the fabric. It filled up like a vacuum pack, forming itself into a WEDGE shape under her foot.

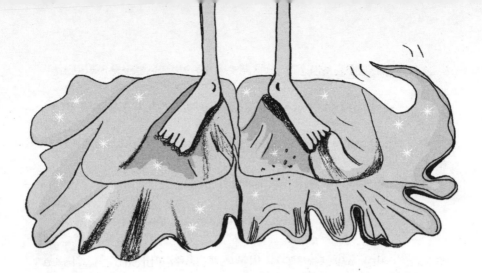

"Our wedges are temperature sensitive and can react to your mood and surroundings. Imagine you're getting irritated because you're stuck in a long queue. They will vibrate gently to soothe your tensions away,"

Phillip explained as the wedges began to pulse all over, giving Parminda's feet a massage.

"I NEVER queue. What else can they do?"

Wendy snapped.

"They also turn any foot moisture into scented water that collects over the surface in tiny amounts. You can sit in the garden with your feet up and beautiful birds and butterflies will be drawn to you."

"Allow us to demonstrate," Parminda said and looked over to Phillip, who released a few butterflies and tiny birds. They fluttered in the air before coming to rest on Parminda's wedges. The birds tweeted and there was a general feeling of sweetness and well-being all around.

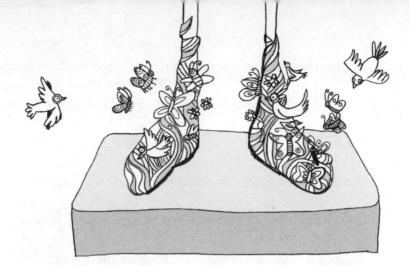

"GHASTLY! Who wants INSECTS or BIRDS attacking your feet?

That wouldn't make me feel calm.

I'd be **FURIOUS!**

I've. Seen. **ENOUGH!"**

Wendy screeched. Her voice had the birds

and butterflies scattering out of the window. **"Now."** She turned

to Ivor, and that nasty smile curled her mouth again.

"YOU. IVOR FOOT. WHAT do you have for me?"

Ivor took a deep breath.

"The thing is, Ms Wedge, Mr Creeper said YOU already have my WEDGES?"

There was a silence while she watched him. Then Mr Creeper took two slightly battered, damp camera wedges from his bag and dropped them on the table in front of Ivor.

"Oh! What happened?" Ivor asked, picking some wet leaves off the bashed-up shoes.

"What happened, Mr Foot, is that Mr Creeper kindly decided to TEST RUN them for you."

"He took my shoes?" asked Ivor.

"MY shoes, Mr Foot. Remember, anything YOU make is mine. And while he was wearing MY shoes he managed to record something VERY interesting. Didn't you, Mr Creeper?"

Mr Creeper nodded as much as he could with his sore neck.

"Is there something you want to SHARE with me, Ivor? Anything at all?" Wendy asked in a VERY menacing way. Before Ivor could say anything, Mr Creeper turned on the camera wedges and a faint, grainy picture projected on to the wall. Everyone fell silent to listen, but the sound was scratchy. (That's putting it mildly.)

Sehoeibfoqeibfqbd cjnns bljb fly lnlspifjn djpwoj dpojepf pqpirbf fky.

"It really does get better," Mr Creeper said.

"I hope so – for YOUR sake," Wendy told him. Ivor went quiet. This wasn't going well.

Mr Creeper turned the camera wedge **OFF ...** and then **ON** as Wendy sighed heavily. This time, the sound was crystal clear.

"Let me get this straight – you TOOK my flying shoes from my workshop. THEN you used them to FLY to the BRAND NEW Wedge Town sign and paint a heart over it?"

"It looks so much nicer now, Dad. You should see it."

"HOW did you even know where to FIND the shoes? I can't hide anything from you two, can I?"

"Not really..."

Ivor cringed.

This was **BAD**.

"IVOR FOOT, you have been FOUND OUT!"

Wendy **FUMED.**

Mr Creeper walked towards Ivor and held up a long TUBE in

front of him, then slowly began pulling it apart to reveal …

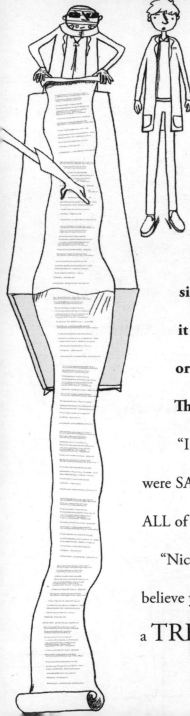

… a piece of paper.

He rolled the paper out on to the desk

in front of him. It was so long it tumbled

off the end and kept on going.

Wendy pointed at it.

"THIS is the contract that YOU

signed and have broken. SEE? RIGHT here

it states that any shoes you have made now

or in the past ALL belong to Wendy Wedge.

That's ME."

"I haven't broken my contract – the flying shoes

were SALLY'S, not mine. SHE made them. You have

ALL of MY shoes," Ivor tried to explain.

"Nice try, Ivor. But Sally isn't here, so why would I

believe you? AND we have MORE evidence that you are

a TREACHEROUS LIAR."

She was definitely enjoying herself now.

"Ivor Foot, **YOU** are in possession

of **FLYING SHOES and OTHER**

FOOTWEAR that is ILLEGAL.

You've broken WEDGE TOWN LAW

not once, but TWICE," Wendy told him.

Chief Inspector Slingback nodded in

agreement.

"That's right, Ms Wedge, he has.

Mr Creeper has PROOF."

Ivor tried to stick up for himself.

"But I—"

"SHUT it, IVOR."

Wendy stomped her foot again, then gestured

for Mr Creeper to continue. He reached under his desk ...

and very slowly brought out ...

... a pair of fluffy white slippers.

Mr Creeper placed them on the table and

patted their fluffiness.

Wendy lurched backwards dramatically,

as the mere SIGHT of slippers made her

feel faint with DISGUST.

"These ... ILLEGAL THINGS

were found in your house, Ivor Foot. What have you got to say

ABOUT THAT?" Wendy demanded.

"They're not mine, Ms Wedge. I've never seen them before!

SOMEONE must have put them there.

It's a slipper SET-up!"

Ivor tried to explain.

"Fluff and nonsense –

get them out of my sight!" Wendy

shrieked like they were the WORST things she'd ever seen.

189

Officer Bunion began to read Ivor his rights.
"Ivor Foot, you are under arrest
for the possession of illegal
slippers AND for breaking
your contract with Wendy

Wedge by not handing over the FLYING shoes."

Wendy interrupted him. **"IF I don't get what I want, YOU'RE**

going to Footwear Prison for a very long time. Take him away."

"WAIT! You CAN'T do this!" Ivor shouted.

"I can do ANYTHING I want, Ivor. I OWN this town,"

Wendy corrected him.

"But the kids need me. I need them. They can't be left alone! They've

already lost their mother!" pleaded Ivor. But Wendy just smiled nastily.

"Well, I'm sure we can find a way round that. After all, they

are little criminals too. They dropped red paint on my Walter.

Vandalized the Wedge Town sign, which is public property. Both

criminal offences."

"It was an accident! The flying shoes still need WORK – they went WONKY in the air. It wasn't their fault, the paint just spilled out," Ivor tried to explain.

"Did EVERYONE hear that? A room full of witnesses just heard you confess that your HORRID children viciously ATTACKED my Walter!" Wendy shrieked triumphantly.

Walter stood up and added pompously, "RUBY and BEAR need to be punished, Mother!"

"You can't do this," Ivor shouted desperately.

"I can," Wendy told him.

"You can't," Ivor replied.

"I can too!" Wendy said, like a toddler having a tantrum.

Betty Boot could see the WHOLE situation was going very badly for Ivor and decided to do something about it while she still could. Quietly, she began to edge her way towards the door.

If she could slip out of Wendy's office before anyone spotted her, there was a chance she could find the Foot kids and keep them safe.

Luckily for Betty, Wendy's GRATING voice was loud enough to cover up the sound of the door sliding open and shut.

"I CAN do what I WANT! HAND OVER THE FLYING SHOES OR YOU WILL NEVER WORK IN THIS TOWN OR ANY OTHER TOWN AGAIN. I COULD have you LOCKED UP FOR A VERY VERY VERY LONG TIME!" Wendy shouted.

"YEAH! SO THERE!" Walter added

(when there was really no need to).

"Fine," Ivor said quietly. "You win, Ms Wedge. You can have the FLYING shoes. BUT there's something you should know. Those shoes aren't ready yet. They wobble around in the air, and I'm the only person who can fix them. So if you want to win **THE GOLDEN SHOE AWARD,** you need to DROP these stupid slipper charges." He took a deep breath. "And leave Ruby and Bear out of this."

"Just PUT them ALL in PRISON, Mother!" Walter shouted excitedly.

Wendy held up her hand for silence.

"Oh, Ivor," she said coldly. **"Don't you realize I could get ANYONE in this room to fix the shoes? Even Mr Creeper could do it."**

Mr Creeper whispered in Wendy's ear.

"What do you mean, you don't know how they work? What kind of an assistant ARE you?" Wendy asked and Mr Creeper shrugged his shoulders. It was better to tell her now. Phillip Flop bravely stepped forward and spoke up.

"Ms Wedge, Ivor's telling the truth. He IS the only person who could fix the shoes. None of us know how they work."

Chief Inspector Slingback cleared her throat. "Also, Ms Wedge, I just remembered – we might need a proper trial of some kind before putting anyone in prison." Wendy looked irritated.

"Really? Oh, how BORING." She turned her back to Ivor. **"All right – hand the shoes over and then you get one chance to FIX them."**

"Yes, Ms Wedge," Ivor assured her.

"But first you have to promise

to leave my kids out of all this?"

"Don't make me lose my temper," Wendy muttered.

"Please, you have to promise." Ivor held out his little finger.

"What are you doing?" Wendy snapped.

"I'm asking you to make a pinky promise," Ivor explained.

"This is ridiculous! Who on EARTH

does a pinky promise?"

She looked around the room.

Officer T-Bar put up his hand.

       "Sometimes I do."

"It does kind of work," Office Bunion agreed.

Parminda Platform and Terry Trainer both nodded as well.

Ivor took this opportunity to fill Wendy's thoughts with visions of flying. "Ms Wedge, imagine the scene – you're flying effortlessly above everyone's heads. The judges are STUNNED by your brilliance. ALL the people in other shoe-making towns and cities who LAUGHED at your wooden flying shoes that never got off the ground have to watch as the judges award YOU **THE GOLDEN SHOE AWARD."** (Wendy's expression became dreamy and Ivor knew she was imagining flying triumphantly over an awestruck crowd.)

"Think of it. NO ONE will ever be able to laugh behind your back again," he continued.

"People laughed at me?" Wendy turned to Mr Creeper. **"Is that true?"**

He didn't look her in the eye, but did a "maybe a little" sign with his hand – which was enough to set Wendy OFF again.

"HOW DARE they? I'll show those terrible tiny towns who's WHO."

"Exactly, Ms Wedge. Think of the satisfaction you'll get from

showing places like **Shoehampton**, Trainerville, Little Toehampton,

BIG Toehampton, Shoecastle, Walking-on-Sea and

Bootchester … that YOU have the flying shoes they could only

DREAM OF. They'll be DAZZLED by YOUR fearless flying."

Ivor took a breath…

"Just remember: you have to leave

Ruby and Bear alone. A pinky

promise HAS to be kept."

Wendy GLARED at him.

"Hmmmmmm…"

"MOTHER! Don't do it! It's a TRICK!" Walter shouted.

"It's not a trick, Walter. It's ASSURANCE that we'll both keep our ends of the bargain," Ivor said. He stretched out his little finger and wiggled it.

VERY reluctantly, Wendy stuck out her little finger.

"Pinky ... promise," she muttered, and snatched her hand back as fast as she could.

"NOW TELL ME WHERE the FLYING SHOES ARE!"

"Under the round table in my secret workshop. You'll need to press the tiles down in a special order to open it up – I'll write it down."

"I KNEW that table looked suspicious!"

Wendy snatched the code from Ivor and handed it to the SHOE POLICE.

"GO! And, Mr Creeper, take him away!"

Wendy GLARED at Ivor.

"You can't!" Ivor shouted.

"Oh, I CAN – THIS is my insurance that YOU won't be leaving this building until I have the FLYING SHOES and **THE GOLDEN SHOE AWARD** in my hands." Ivor tried to protest, but it was too late. With the dogs growling around his feet, Mr Creeper led Ivor away.

Wendy turned to the others.

"What are you lot all GAWPING at? He's a SHOE CRIMINAL! No more TIPTOEING AROUND! Get back to work, all of you – or I'll arrest YOU TOO!" They all shuffled out of the room.

Chief Inspector Slingback took the code for the table and the officers left to fetch the flying shoes. Ivor was escorted away by Mr Creeper and the GROWLING DOGS. Wendy followed to remind Ivor that…

BYE

"No flying shoes means no

GOLDEN SHOE AWARD –

and NO escape for you, EVER!"

"MOTHER! Don't forget you promised to punish the children!" Walter reminded her.

"Of course! I always keep my promises, Walter." Wendy smiled and THAT made Ivor MAD.

"Leave my kids OUT of this! You are a lia—"

Mr Creeper shoved Ivor into a small room and locked the door.

"Left, Right – stay alert and on guard," Mr Creeper ordered them.

NO!

grrrr

Wendy rubbed her hands together. Her plan was working out

nicely.

"I'll be WAITING for the flying shoes in my office, Mr Creeper

– DON'T LET ME DOWN,"

she said, fixing him with a STERN STARE.

"WHAT Mother said,"

Walter added, and STAMPED his foot

down accidentally on Mr Creeper's foot.

Mr Creeper waited until Wendy

and Walter were out of sight...

Hmmmm

GENIUS

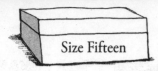

Size Fifteen

Betty Boot had BRAVELY made it out of Wendy's office. She dumped her white coat in the locker room. "Stay calm," she told herself. She needed to get Ruby and Bear to safety. Wendy was out of **CONTROL!** Threatening to put everyone in PRISON was the last straw or Betty. She was going to find the kids and take them somewhere safe. Who knew what Wendy would do next?

(Something ROTTEN, that's for sure.)

Betty slipped out of the WOW building, walking fast. She had almost made it past the guards when they STOPPED her. "Ms Boot?" they said as their dogs growled at her feet.

"Yes?" she asked nervously.

"With **THE GOLDEN SHOE AWARD** tomorrow, we're stepping up security. Please wear your pass next time, OK?"

"I'm sorry, I will. I was in a hurry."

Betty waved and they waved back and lifted the barrier – which was a big relief.

It was a short walk to the school where Betty could see the children were already playing outside at break.

Good timing, she thought.

BUT getting inside the school grounds without being seen was going to be tricky. UNTIL Betty spotted a loose wooden fence panel. "Perfect," she whispered and lifted it up. Betty squeezed herself in, then hid behind a large pot plant. She peered out through the leaves looking for the kids. It wasn't long before her daughter Chelsea ran past. Betty did a loud "Pssssssttttttt!" to attract her attention.

Chelsea stopped. Was the plant talking?

"Pssst – Chelsea! It's me, Mum. Don't turn round."

Chelsea turned round and peered at her mum in confusion.

"I'll explain EVERYTHING later. Right now I need you to go and find Ruby and Bear and bring them back here, fast. Can you do that?"

Chelsea nodded yes.

"Are we leaving school early?" she asked hopefully.

"Yes. Go quickly and try NOT to bring attention to yourself, OK?"

Betty said then motioned for her to GO.

"BEAR AND RUBY FOOT! WHERE ARE YOU? COME HERE QUICKLY!"

Chelsea's voiced BOOMED across the playground.

Betty shook her head. Chelsea kept shouting until she found them

sitting on a bench. Unfortunately, Chloe Clog

and Willie Winklepicker were there too,

bothering them. Chelsea kept her distance

and tried to get just Ruby and Bear's attention …

206

… the best way she could.

"Oh, look! Our friend wants us to come over. Time to go," Ruby told Chloe and Willie.

But Willie and Chloe were both in a MOOD and wouldn't let them pass.

"What's the hurry?" Chloe said, LOOMING OVER Ruby.

"Can you move, please?" Bear asked nicely.

"Not until you show us your WEDGES. Walter told us to check you don't have any more illegal gadgets inside them," Willie snarled.

"YEAH – you two think you're SO SPECIAL when you're not," Chloe added.

"Show us your SHOES. NOW!" Willie demanded.

"They're just the same as yours, leave us alone," Bear told them sternly.

"IF you've got GADGETS hidden inside, we'll tell Walter, who'll tell his MUM and you'll both get into LOTS MORE trouble," Chloe sneered and leaned really CLOSE to Ruby's face.

"Eeewwwwwww… There's something on your nose," Ruby said, frowning.

"Oh…" Chloe tried to check, then realized Ruby was joking. "You're not funny," she snapped.

"You are, though!" Ruby laughed and Chloe glared.

"Let's see your shoes! OR ELSE!" Willie said, STAMPING his foot down really hard.

"You've been hanging out with Walter Wedge for too long," Bear told him.

"HEY! Walter's my BEST friend!" Willie snapped back.

"And MINE," Chloe added.

"Walter's not a REAL friend – you'll see," Ruby told them.

"No, YOU'LL see," Chloe sneered.

"YEAH – you'll both be SORRY."

Willie grimaced, trying to be extra tough.

(All the time Chelsea was still FRANTICALLY trying to get

Ruby and Bear to come over.)

"See you later, Williegator!" Ruby said as she and Bear pushed past.

"HEY – come back here!" Willie shouted.

"We should follow them…" Chloe said.

"Nah – let's find someone smaller to annoy instead." Willie

pointed to a girl walking past (who sensibly ignored them both).

"If Walter was here, she wouldn't

ignore us," Chloe sighed.

"No one would," Willie agreed. (It was true…)

"Oi!"

Can't stop!

Ruby and Bear finally joined Chelsea, who said:

"My mum told me to get you – it's urgent. Come quickly!"

They ran back to Betty (who was still hiding in the plant).

Relieved to see all three of the kids heading her way,

Betty gave them a hug and told them quickly, "Your

dad's OK, but we need to get you somewhere safe RIGHT NOW."

"Away from Wendy Wedge?" Bear asked.

"YES – come on, follow me." Betty held up the broken fence

panel so they could squeeze back through.

"Does this have something to do with the flying shoes?" Ruby

whispered, trying to keep up with Betty.

"A little – but everything will be fine, I promise," Betty replied,

sounding more hopeful than she felt.

They got away just in time. As they slipped under the fence, the

shoe police arrived at the school gates with STRICT instructions to

find those FOOT children.

It turned out that Foot was a popular surname in **Shoe Town,** and it took the shoe police a while to work out that Ruby and Bear Foot had already left the building.

Betty knew some good shortcuts that got them back to the **Shoebox Estate** without being spotted.

"We'll keep you out of Wendy's sight until it's dark," Betty told Ruby and Bear reassuringly.

Chelsea tugged on her mum's arm. "Look who's there," she whispered.

It was Mr Creeper.

"Quick, HIDE!" Betty said as they pressed up against the wall.

He headed into the Foots' house as two police cars pulled up outside Betty's house.

"There's shoe police EVERYWHERE. We can't stay here," Betty sighed.

"What do we do now?" asked Bear. This day was turning into a NIGHTMARE.

"We could hide in the chip shop?" Chelsea suggested, as she was hungry.

"Not right now," Betty told her wearily.

Bear looked at Ruby. He could tell what was going through her mind.

"Don't even think about it."

"I wasn't going to sing – I was going to say, we should go to Bert's, he'll hide us," Ruby suggested.

"That's a GREAT idea! Well done, Ruby – let's go."

Betty took their hands and they headed to Bert's shoe shop as fast as they could.

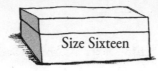

Size Sixteen

Betty looked around to check no one was following them, then opened the door to Bert's Brogues. A bell went PING to tell Bert that he had visitors.

"Coming," he called out from his workshop at the back. Ruby pointed to the PROTEST SIGNS in the window.

"I did that one!" she said, smiling.

Betty admired Bert for putting up a fight against World of Wedge taking over his shop. She knew he'd want to help them. Bert had been busy putting the finishing touches to an excellent pair of hand-made brogues and was pleased and surprised to see Betty, Chelsea and the Foot kids all standing there.

"Hello, lovely people!" He grinned. "What can I do for you? Are Wendy's 'wonderful' new school WOWs hurting your feet? Or has school just finished early today?"

Betty wasted no time telling Bert all about Wendy Wedge getting her horrible hands on Ivor's flying shoes.

"These two need a safe place to hide," Betty told him. "And we're hoping you can help."

"Of course! That Wendy Wedge is a nasty piece of work!" Bert said crossly. "She's been trying to close me down for ages. Mr Creeper leaves her dogs outside my shop to scare my customers away. BUT I've been feeding them sneaky sausages so they don't bother anyone." Bert laughed. "They're too FULL to move and Mr Creeper has no idea."

"Good for you, Bert," Betty smiled.

"That's so funny!" Ruby said and picked up a pair of hand-made boots with a secret compartment in the heel.

"Your shoes look really comfy," Chelsea told him.

"Well Bert is a MASTER shoemaker. But right now we need to keep Ruby and Bear out of sight," Betty reminded everyone, and ushered them into the

workshop at the back. It was nice to sit down

after all the rushing around, and Betty

needed some time to think.

"I want to be a master shoemaker one day," Ruby told everyone, looking around in awe.

"You'll need to be an apprentice for three years first, though Bert did it in two," Bear explained.

"How do you know that?" Bert asked, slightly surprised.

"You told me once and I'm good at remembering stuff," Bear said.

"He really is – it can be annoying," Ruby added.

"I'm not the only master shoemaker here. Betty, you've always made wonderful shoes."

"Wendy doesn't think so – she wasn't impressed with my music wedges!" Betty told him.

"What does SHE know?" Bert said crossly.

"She knows there's a chance of her winning **THE GOLDEN SHOE AWARD** tomorrow. IF Ivor can fix the flying shoes," said Betty.

"I hope he can figure it out FAST, for his sake," said Bert.

Bear and Ruby looked worried.

"Who's hungry?" Bert asked, to distract them.

"ME!" Ruby, Bear and Chelsea put up their hands.

"We can't stay, Chelsea." Betty sighed.

"Pleeeeeease can I have some cake?" Chelsea pleaded.

"We really need to get back to the estate to keep an eye on Ruby and Bert's home. We can let them know when the shoe police have gone and the coast is clear," Betty explained. She hugged Ruby and Bear.

"Everything will be fine, I promise. We'll get you home when it's dark later."

Bert put some cake in a bag and gave it to Chelsea, which cheered her up.

"Thanks, Bert!" Betty smiled and hugged him too.

"What are old friends for? Us master shoemakers need to stick together."

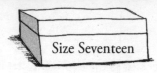

Bert closed up the shop and put a sign on the door.

He hoped that would keep everyone away for a while. Ruby and

Bear sat at the table as Bert put out some more food: bread and

butter, cheese, a jar of lemon curd, sausages, olives, a sponge cake

and some tinned peaches in a bowl.

"Thanks for this, Bert," said Bear. "I hope Dad's OK."

"Me too. Stupid Wendy Wedge," Ruby replied, helping herself to

some cake.

"I'm sure he's going to be fine. Sorry about the odd mixture of

food!" Bert apologized.

"We don't mind," Bear said, eating some cheese while Ruby

helped herself to a sausage.

"It's not fair — Wendy shouldn't win the award for Mum's flying shoes," Ruby said in between mouthfuls.

"I agree. In all my shoemaking years, I've never even got CLOSE to making a pair of flying shoes. I wouldn't know where to start," said Bert. "Your dad never told me they existed — he's fantastic at keeping secrets. I wonder how Wendy found out?"

Ruby and Bear looked at each other. "It's all our fault," Ruby said miserably. "Dad kept them safe in his shoe workshop. But I woke up one night and saw him flying around the kitchen in them. Bear was asleep — snoring his head off."

"I wasn't snoring," Bear protested.

"You were too. Anyway," Ruby carried on, "we borrowed the shoes to FLY up and paint over the new Wedge Town sign — I used the red paint you gave us, Bert!"

"YOU two did that?" Bert asked, surprised.

Ruby and Bear nodded enthusiastically.

"BUT the shoes wobbled in the air and GUESS who the paint spilled on to?" Ruby asked.

"Wendy?" asked Bert with a shudder.

"Almost – it was Walter. He kind of saw us flying away," Ruby sighed.

"That's why Mr Creeper is in our house now. He's looking for the shoes," Bear explained, then put a dollop of lemon curd on to a tinned peach slice.

lemon curd

tinned peach

"Is that nice?" Ruby asked curiously.

"I'll tell you in a moment…" He popped it in his mouth. "Mmmmm, sweet but nice," Bear said.

"Dad says the only thing Wendy Wedge cares about is her wedges and WINNING **THE GOLDEN SHOE AWARD,**" Ruby told Bert.

"Your dad's right. The humiliation of losing the last two awards hasn't helped. Everyone knew her WEIGHTLESS WONDER WEDGES were a disaster."

"They were the lowest scoring shoes ever in the history of the awards. And she's lost the last THREE," Bear said, correcting Bert.

"That's made her more DESPERATE to win at any cost. I don't like the way Wendy is taking over EVERYTHING in this town. It's not right. Let's hope Mr Creeper doesn't find the shoes," Bert said, getting even more cross. "Dad's secret workshop is FULL of stuff to hunt through. They *COULD* still be there."

"Let's go back and check?" Bear suggested.

"We could enter **THE GOLDEN SHOE AWARD** with flying shoes then!" Ruby was getting excited about that idea.

"I'm not sure that would work. We don't want to make things worse for your dad, do we?" Bert said.

"There MUST be something we can do?" Ruby asked, trying a slice of tinned peach and lemon curd herself.

"What if Dad doesn't manage to fix the shoes? If Wendy doesn't win the award, I'm worried she won't let him go," said Ruby.

"And even if she DOES, she'll probably keep him locked up making shoes for her for EVER," said Bear.

"We have to do something," said Ruby. "It's not fair for Wendy to win with Mum's shoes."

"You're right," said Bear, a glint in his eye. "It's time someone stopped Wendy. I think we should make a plan. But first, have some more bread."

Bear took a slice while Ruby tried an olive for the very first time.

(And the very last)

*Foot note: she was right to be worried.

Ruby's anti-olive face.

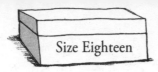

Size Eighteen

Night fell. Eventually the phone rang: it was Betty to say that the shoe police and Mr Creeper had left the **Shoebox Estate.** Bert packed up the leftover sausages with some more cake for Ruby and Bear to take with them.

"Are you ready, kids?" he asked.

"We are SO ready," Bear said.

"Fingers crossed Mr Creeper will have failed and the flying shoes will still be there," Ruby added. They slipped out into the night and made it safely to their house. "We'll need to be quick in case anyone comes back," Bert whispered.

Ruby and Bear followed him to the front door, which was already open.

Inside the house …

... it was a MESS.

There was stuff all over the place. Worse still, Sally's round table in the kitchen had been FORCED open and some of the beautifully painted tiles were cracked.

"I can fix them – don't worry," Bert reassured Ruby and Bear.

"That's Dad's workshop," Ruby told him.

"Very clever," Bert said, admiring the secret entrance.

They climbed down the ladder, and straight away saw an empty wooden box on the floor.

"The flying shoes were probably in here," Bert sighed.

"But we'll keep looking, just in case." Ruby had never seen inside the workshop before. It was full of fascinating objects. She crouched down to a low shelf and found a collection of interesting-looking books. She took one out that was tied up with a faded ribbon, and was about to read the title when Bert said they should double-check upstairs.

Ruby slipped it under her jumper, and while Bear and

Bert looked round the rest of the house, she took it

back out for a read. On the cover in perfect

handwriting, it said:

Sally Sandal's
Book of Shoe Designs
and Dreams.

"It's Mum's," Ruby whispered, then untied the ribbon and

opened the book. On every page of the slightly yellow paper was a

detailed drawing of some very different types of shoes. Each design

had tiny handwritten instructions next to it.

"Wow…" Ruby was fascinated by it all.

She could hear Bear telling her to hurry up. Ruby closed the book, then squeezed it inside her bag before joining them.

Bert was standing in their bedroom and shaking his head. "Oh my, Mr Creeper and the shoe police really messed up your room too," he sighed.

Bear laughed, "No, this is what it always looks like in here. Ruby's just very messy. She has a LOT of stuff, especially dungarees."

"You're messier than me, and I *like* dungarees. I'm putting on my lucky pair right now," Ruby said.

"We could use all the help we can get," Bert said, then suddenly STOPPED talking, putting his hand up to his mouth.

"Shhh! Don't move a muscle," he whispered. They all FROZE. SOMETHING was making the floorboards creak outside.

Shoo leaped OUT

and gave them all a

FRIGHT!

"AGH!" Bert screamed.

"It's only Shoo," Ruby said. She picked the

cat up. "Calm down…"

"I'm trying," Bert sighed.

"I was talking to Shoo," Ruby said.

YOWWWL

"We should bring Shoo with us to keep her safe," suggested Bear.

"Good idea," Bert agreed. "Now grab what you need and let's get to Betty's." Bert went to the kitchen window to check the coast was still clear.

Ruby changed into her lucky dungarees while Bear took one more look round for the flying shoes. They were definitely gone.

"We'll have to go out of the back door now – there's a lady talking to the shoe police officer outside," warned Bert.

"Is she holding a walking stick?" Bear asked.

"Yes."

"Mrs Court," Ruby and Bear both said together.

"She is super nosy," Ruby explained.

"Hopefully she'll keep the officer busy," Bear added.

They sneaked out of the back door and made it to Betty's without anyone seeing them.

Chelsea wasted no time in helping Ruby and Bear get settled. Betty had put a couple of sleeping bags in her room, which was a bit of a squash, but they didn't mind. No one had much space on the **Shoebox Estate.**

"Thanks for looking after them, Bert," Betty said, handing him some tea. "No flying shoes, though?"

"Gone. Mr Creeper must have given them to Wendy by now," Bert said as he sipped his tea.

"I'm trying not to worry the kids, but it's not easy," Betty whispered to Bert.

The full realization of what Wendy was up to was REALLY starting to sink in.

"If Wendy does use the flying shoes to win the award tomorrow, things will never be the same again," Bert said dramatically, shaking his head.

"What do you mean?" Ruby asked, listening in to their conversation.

"Nothing to worry about. After your dad gets home, she'll just BRAG about the award for ever," Betty said, doing her best to play things down.

"And that's not all… Mark my words, no other town or city will EVER be allowed to make flying shoes. The World of Wedge will take over EVERY single shoe shop. We'll be forced to wear her big, clumpy wedges ALL the time just because SHE likes them. Wendy will use the flying shoes for WORLD SHOE domination. She's already banned SLIPPERS. That's just a start. There'll be no room for shops like mine any more. It's only a matter of time before she does SOMETHING SERIOUSLY sneaky to close me down."

Bert took a breath and stopped. He could tell from everyone's expressions he was getting a little worked up.

"OR, she might not win and everything will stay the same, so

don't listen to me," Bert said, trying to calm down.

(A bit late...)

"Why didn't you and Betty ever try making flying shoes, Bert?"

asked Ruby.

"I was wondering that too," Bear said.

"I did try," said Bert. "But I could

never get them to work.

It was too difficult. Your mum,

Sally, really was a genius! It must've taken her years to get them

right."

"That's true. Every shoemaker's DREAM was to invent the first pair of flying shoes," Betty added.

"Remember Wendy's Wooden Wonders? They never even got off the ground!" Bert laughed.

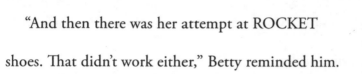

"And then there was her attempt at ROCKET shoes. That didn't work either," Betty reminded him.

"They only stayed up for thirty-five seconds before they fell back down," Bear told them. He always knew good SHOE facts.

weee

ARRRRGH!

"I really wanted to make shoes that could fly. I just never knew WHERE to start," said Betty.

"But what if you had something that SHOWED

you EXACTLY how to make them?

Could you do it then?"

Ruby wondered.

"You mean like a manual?" asked Bert.

"It would have to be VERY detailed," said Betty. "But yes, probably."

"I'll be back in a second," Ruby told them and went to get her bag.

"What's she up to?" Bear said suspiciously. Ruby came back with her bag and took out the BIG book.

"Where did you get that?" Bear asked.

"Dad's workshop," said Ruby. She carefully put the book on the table. "It's Mum's notebook. It's full of diagrams and notes."

They gathered round to take a closer look.

"I recognize your mother's beautiful handwriting," Betty told them.

Bert peered closely at the detailed drawings. "Oh my, THIS is amazing. You're right, everything's HERE – all the instructions are in this book. Your mum was SO clever! This is perfect."

Bert was very impressed.

"So could you make flying shoes NOW from Mum's plans?"
Bear asked.

Bert considered the diagram thoughtfully. "Maybe," he said. "It might be possible, with the help of another master shoemaker." He looked at Betty.

"Go on, Mum – make the flying shoes!" said Chelsea.

"You could ENTER **THE GOLDEN SHOE AWARD!"** Ruby said.

"RUBY, you're a genius!" Bear said.

"Finally, we agree on something!"

"Imagine the LOOK on Wendy's face." Bear laughed.

"It would be worth it just for that," Betty agreed.

"But do we have enough time?" Bert asked.

Betty suddenly stopped reading. "OH NO!" she said.

"What's wrong?" Bert asked.

"I can't help you, Bert. You'll have to make them by yourself," she said.

"Why?" he asked.

"Because I have exactly the SAME contract as Ivor. All the shoes I make belong to Wendy and WOW. If I even help you make the flying shoes, they'll belong to her."

"Is that legal?" Bert said.

"In Wedge Town it is. Wendy does what she wants."

"How will she know?" Ruby wondered.

"Trust me – she'll find out." The smile left Bert's face. Without Betty's help, making the flying shoes would be very difficult.

"You can do it, Bert." Ruby told him.

"Pleeeeeaasse, Bert! I really want to fly!" Chelsea asked nicely.

"It's a lot of fun…" Bear said.

"It really is," Ruby agreed.

"You could SELL them in your shop. Flying shoes would be SO popular, Bert. You and Dad – together you'd make a FORTUNE!" Bear said.

"Wendy couldn't shut you down then," Ruby added.

"They've got a point, Bert. What do you think?" Betty asked him.

"There's not much time. I'd HAVE to work ALL through the night to have a chance, and even then…" Bert said, thinking aloud. "But YES, I'll do it. It's about time we stood up to Wendy Wedge."

"GO, BERT!" Ruby and Bear shouted, and Chelsea cheered.

"Right, I'd better get back to my workshop and get started. I just hope Ivor would be pleased about all this," Bert said.

"He will be pleased we're fighting back. This could change everything," Betty said.

"It's US against World of Wedge," Bear told them.

"It's SHOE WARS!" said Ruby proudly.

Betty carefully put Sally's book into a brown paper bag and gave it to Bert.

"I won't let you all down," Bert said, determined to do his best.

Wendy Wedge wasn't going to WIN this award with shoes that didn't belong to HER.

They all watched as Bert slipped out of the back door into the night. Bert walked fast, clutching the precious book under his arm and keeping his head down. He took a corner at speed and bumped RIGHT into…

Mr Creeper.

The book slipped from under his arm and FELL on to the ground.

"Look where you're going, will you?" Mr Creeper told him sharply. He was still sore from the stings.

Bert hurried to pick the book up before Mr Creeper could see it.

"I'm so sorry, I was miles away," Bert told him while trying to get the book back into the bag. His fingers didn't seem to work and he dropped

 it AGAIN. Mr Creeper

scowled – Bert

was holding them up.

"Sorry, it's way past my bedtime. I really must … fly!" Bert managed to splutter. He clutched the book to his chest and ran off down the road.

INSTANTLY, Bert wished he hadn't said THAT word. "Why did I say FLY?" he muttered to himself.

Mr Creeper stood and watched him go. "Why is Bert in such a

hurry?" he wondered. Bert seemed nervous and jumpy. It got

Mr Creeper thinking that Bert might be up to something.

This took his mind off his now very itchy foot. But not for long.

"When will this stop itching?"* he muttered.

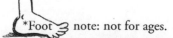
*Foot note: not for ages.

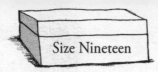

Size Nineteen

Bert got away from Mr Creeper as fast as he could. He hadn't seen the book, which was a relief. Bert needed to get busy shoemaking (the flying kind). Back inside the shop he quickly locked all the doors and pulled down the blinds. Then, safe in his workshop, he began to read all of Sally's instructions. They were clear, with helpful diagrams. To keep up his energy, Bert found himself strangely drawn to eating a tinned peach with some lemon curd on it* – and instantly regretted it.

"What was I thinking?" he asked himself before automatically eating another one.

It was going to be a very,

VERY long night.

*Bert's tinned peach
and lemon curd face*

 Foot note: don't try this at home.

Bert – working super hard.

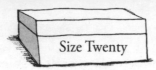

Betty put the kids to bed and tucked them in, hoping they'd get some sleep.

"When will Wendy let Dad go?" Ruby asked her.

"Soon – he just needs to fix the wobble in the shoes," Betty replied. "I will go into WOW early tomorrow and make sure he's OK. I'm going to stand up to Wendy as well."

Chelsea went to sleep, but Ruby and Bear lay awake for ages, thinking about everything that had happened.

"Bear, are you awake?" Ruby whispered.

"No."

"Yes, you are."

"Joke."

"What if Wendy doesn't let Dad go?" she said in a small, scared voice.

"She can't keep him there for ever. It's against the law," Bear replied, which didn't make Ruby feel any better. She got up and took a peek through the window. She could see the big W building through the blinds. Ruby whispered, "Dad is in there somewhere, and…"

"And what…?" Bear asked.

"And we need to do something. What if Wendy gets super mad and throws a WOBBLY? She doesn't care about the law. I don't trust her. She might even HURT Dad. We've already lost Mum. We can't lose Dad too."

Bear sat up and looked at his sister bravely.

"You're right, Ruby, we need to get into WOW and rescue Dad. But how?"

"I can help you," Chelsea whispered.

(She'd been awake and listening the whole time).

"I know where my mum keeps her pass."

"We don't want you to get in trouble,"
Bear said.

"If it was my mum locked up, I'd do the same," said Chelsea.
"She was friends with your mum. She'd want to help."

"I miss Mum," said Bear quietly.

"Me too," said Ruby.

The kids lay there in silence for a moment. "Mum wouldn't take any
nonsense from Wendy," Bear told them.

"Exactly – that's why we should do it.
She wouldn't rest until Dad was
rescued and back home," Ruby said.

*Cat air
punch*

Shoo meowed like she agreed too.

"I'll get the pass, but what about the dogs? They'll be snarling
around," Chelsea reminded them.

"Oh yeah, those horrible dogs…" Ruby winced.

Bear and Ruby got dressed and Chelsea handed them a pass for WOW, a backpack each and a choice of masks. "You don't want anyone to recognize you. There's a mouse or a unicorn," she explained.

"Good thinking. I bagsy the mouse," Bear said.

"I wanted the mouse!" Ruby protested.

"OK, you take it." Bear handed it  over. "It suits you better."

"I've put in Bert's sausages too," said Chelsea. "I'll put pillows in your sleeping bags so it looks like you're still there. My mum doesn't need to know you're gone – she'll just worry."

"We're like secret agents," Ruby whispered excitedly.

"It's US against Wendy Wedge – let OPERATION SHOE WARS begin," said Bear, punching the air.

"If you say so," Ruby smiled.

With everything packed up, Chelsea let them out of the back door. "Good luck," she whispered and waved them off.

Ruby and Bear's special bouncy school wedges made running quicker. The **Shoebox Estate** was nice and quiet, and even Mrs Court seemed to be asleep as her curtains weren't twitching like normal. But as they got closer to WOW, things got a LOT busier. There was a long queue of vans and trucks waiting to go through the WOW gates. People were busy working all through the night to set up for

THE GOLDEN SHOE AWARDS and the guards were carefully checking EVERYONE coming in and out.

"Uh-oh," Ruby whispered.

"We might have to think of another way to get in," Bear said quietly. They kept watch from a safe distance while they thought about what to do next.

A van pulled up alongside them and a man got out and opened the back door. It was STUFFED with balloons that nearly flew out. He checked the address and said,

"This must be the place."

LARRY
LACE
BALOONS

"Are you thinking what I'm thinking?" Ruby said to Bear.

"That depends. What are you thinking?"

"The door is still open – we can

hide and get through the gates."

"That's what I was thinking too," Bear told her.

They hopped in the back with the balloons and tried not to

 BURST any as the van drove up to the gates.

The van stopped and the driver began

talking to the guards. "It's **Larry Lace**

delivering balloons for the awards. I should be

on the list."

"Let's check… Oh, yes, here you are. You're very early."

"I'm trying to finish work and get home. It's my daughter's

birthday tomorrow."

"Oh, nice. How old is she then?" the guard asked.

"She's five. Little Tracy Lace."

"Hope she has a good one. Drive round to parking bay three. Have a nice night," the guard said and waved him through.

Bear and Ruby couldn't see each other for balloons.

"As soon as the van stops, we slip out," Ruby whispered. She put her hand on the door to be ready.

"Take a bunch of balloons for cover," Bear suggested.

"OK, let's go!" Ruby moved the balloons away from her face, then counted to three.

"One … two … three … go!"

They leaped out, dragging the massive bunch of balloons between them and trying not to get tangled up.

"Hey, where are you going with those?"

It was Larry Lace.

Ruby and Bear froze.

"We're taking them to **THE GOLDEN SHOE AWARDS** of course," said Bear.

Lenny Lace squinted at them.

"Wendy's orders," said Ruby.

"OK then," said Larry Lace. "Can you sign for them?"

Ruby scribbled down *W Wedge* on the delivery slip and gave it back.

"Thanks for the help. Have a good **GOLDEN SHOE AWARDS.** Who's going to win – any ideas?" he asked.

"We are," murmered Ruby.

"Good for you," said Larry, not really listening.

He hopped back in his van and drove away.

"That's what happens when you wear LUCKY dungarees," Ruby said. She looked down and saw one of the guard dogs GROWLING at her feet.

"Spoke too soon," she whispered.

"Don't move. He wants a balloon," joked Bear.

"He can have all of them," Ruby whispered.

Grrrrrrrrrrr

W.O.W
DOG

Small angry dog

"We need to get inside," Bear hissed.

"You keep him busy!" Ruby told him.

"How?"

"I don't know – talk to him?"

"Nice doggy..." Bear smiled as the dog growled. "Aren't you sweet?" But the dog growled LOUDER.

"Distract him with a balloon. I'll get the door," Ruby suggested, and got out her pass. She shuffled towards the door and waved the pass over the scanner.

BEEP!

BEEP!

The door CLICKED open just in time.

"Grrrrrrrrr."

"GO! QUICKLY!" Ruby shouted at Bear.

"What about the balloons?"

"LEAVE them!"

So he did, sending the little dog into a furious frenzy as the doors closed behind them and ALL the light disappeared.

They were in

complete darkness.

"Where are you?" Ruby asked.

"Here," Bear told her.

"Where?"

"HERE."

They could feel the

corridor walls, but

it was very hard to

see where they

were going.

"At least no one can see us.

That's a good thing,"

Bear whispered.

"I think I know

which way to go.

Follow me,"

Ruby told him and

started to walk…

PING!

ALL THE LIGHTS

WENT ON AND

DAZZLED THEM.

"Movement sensors. Not ideal," Bear said, blinking in the

BRIGHTNESS.

"At least we can SEE now," Ruby told him.

"Look up there," Bear said, pointing at the ceiling. "Cameras.

Masks on before someone recognizes us."

Ruby and Bear made a run for it, activating the movement

sensors as they went. At the end of the corridor there was another

door. Gasping for breath, they took out the pass.

They went through slowly and looked carefully around the

corner.

Grrrrr! Wooof! WOOOF! WOOOF!

"More dogs! Do you think they're looking for us?" Ruby

whispered.

"I don't want to find out. Let's head over there." Bear pointed to

another door. They pressed themselves up against the walls and slid

along slowly, using their pass once more.

BEEP! They were in.

"This pass is VERY useful. Thank you, Chelsea," Ruby said. So

far, everything was going to plan...*

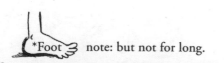

*Foot note: but not for long.

They were inside a big room. There was a large W-shaped desk and the walls were covered with pictures of Wendy, staring down at them fiercely.

"This must be Wendy's office," Bear whispered.

"How can you tell?" Ruby asked.

"Because of…"

"I'm joking. Now, where would Wendy keep Dad?" Ruby asked, looking at the three doors ahead of them.

As they were deciding which way to go, a VERY familiar shadow walked past the frosted glass on the right side of the room.

The sight of Wendy Wedge helped to make up their minds FAST!

"That's Wendy! Quick! Let's get out of here!"

Thump
Thump
Thump

They slipped out of Wendy's office and found themselves in the main part of the World of Wedge building. The workshops were all full of white-coated people looking serious as they finished off their

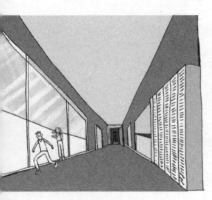

WEDGES for **THE GOLDEN SHOE AWARDS.** Ruby and Bear tiptoed past each window. They popped their heads up and down like meercats, looking out for Dad.

"Why are they still working on those wedges? Wendy has Dad working on the flying shoes," Ruby said.

"Because she's greedy and wants ALL the prizes," Bear whispered, then pointed to a worktop. "Look! There's Dad's camera wedges."

"We could use them NOW to help look for Dad with the camera," Ruby told Bear. They didn't have

to wait long before the door opened and the white-coated shoemakers began to leave.

Bear and Ruby kept quiet and hid behind the door. They slipped into the workshop as the door closed behind them. "HERE – you wear one wedge and I'll wear the other so we'll BOTH have a camera," Ruby suggested. She took a control panel and put it on her wrist, then passed the other one to Bear.

"Ready – let's check. Camera up," Ruby said into her control panel, and made the camera FOCUS on Bear.

"Cooooooeeeee, I can see you! Wave…"she told him.

"Ruby, we don't have time," Bear whispered.

"There's ALWAYS time to annoy you. I'm just testing they work, that's all."

"Good point, let's go," Bear said.

"Where do we start? This building is HUGE," Ruby asked.

"I don't know, but we better hurry," Bear told her.

"We've got to find Dad. He MUST be here somewhere."

They set off down the corridor again.

(Dad was closer than they knew...)

Size Twenty-One

WOOooooFff

WOOOfffff

Wooooofffff

Wooffff

Ivor could hear talking outside the room

he was locked in.

He began rattling the door handle like CRAZY

and yelling, "HEY! Let me out!"

But his shouting only made

the dogs standing guard – Left and Right

– BARK LOUDLY.

Ivor's worrying was now OFF the scale.

Were the kids OK?

How long was Wendy going to keep him for?

And WHO had his flying shoes?

They still needed adjusting to get rid of the WOBBLES.

He'd told Wendy he'd FIX them ready for **THE GOLDEN**

SHOE AWARDS.

But so far, no one had brought them back.

Maybe they didn't believe him? Ivor always kept his promises, unlike Wendy Wedge, who just kept making up random laws to suit herself. Wendy could still CHARGE Ivor with owning the slippers and put him in PRISON.

What was so wrong with slippers anyway?

"I wish I had those flying shoes right now. I'd ESCAPE – FLY out of that door over everyone's heads," Ivor muttered. He was starting to get tired.

"How am I EVER going to get out of here now?" he said to himself.

Ivor was in an impossible situation.*

*Foot note: Or that's what he thought.

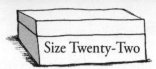

Size Twenty-Two

"We look like SUPERHEROES!" Ruby pointed at the impressively large shadows they were casting in front of them.

"Don't stop – someone might see us," Bear told her – just a little too late. Mr Creeper and Chief Inspector Slingback were WALKING STRAIGHT towards them.

"Do you mean, someone like… them?" Ruby said. "Quick, HIDE!" In a panic, they both ran in different directions.

Bear saw a door and used his pass to get in quickly.

"That was close!" he said, expecting to see Ruby following him. She wasn't there – though something else was….

Gggggrrrrrrrrrrrrrrrr…
GGGrrrrrrrrrrrrrrrrr…

Guard dogs.

"Uh-oh…"

Bear backed up as Left and Right moved closer.

He bumped into a locker, fumbled for the door,

then jumped inside, slamming it SHUT just in time.

The dogs ran at him and were BARKING like crazy.

Things couldn't get any worse, could they? (yes, they

could) Mr Creeper and Chief Inspector Slingback

walked in.

"Pipe down, you two! It's only US," Mr Creeper

said as he walked past the locker. "The code Ivor

gave us for the weird table worked, but the flying

shoes were GONE. We looked everywhere in that

house," Bear heard Mr Creeper say.

"Ivor Foot knows more than he's letting on.

It's time to get TOUGH," said Chief Inspector

Slingback.

GRRRRRRRrrrrrrrrrrrrr

Bear kept watching from inside the locker as they

waved their passes over another door and

pushed it open. For a split-second Bear

caught sight of ...

DAD!

HE WAS IN THAT ROOM!

YES! I've FOUND him!

he thought.

Bear was SO relieved – until he

remembered the dogs.

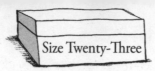

Size Twenty-Three

Chief Inspector Slingback was having a moment.

"YOU LIED TO US, IVOR FOOT! THE FLYING SHOES WEREN'T there! WHAT HAVE YOU DONE WITH THEM, IVOR? WE NEED to FIND them FAST or Wendy will be **unbearable!**"

"You mean MORE unbearable," Ivor corrected him.

"Think of your CHILDREN, Ivor. No **GOLDEN SHOE AWARD** means not seeing your kids for a VERY LONG time," Mr Creeper reminded him.

"Are you SURE you went to the right house?" Ivor asked.

"YES! OF COURSE WE DID!" roared the Chief Inspector, then paused and turned to Mr Creeper. "We did – didn't we?"

"I think so…" Wendy's assistant said.

"Did you REALLY?" Ivor said.

"YES! Stop making it OUR fault! WHERE are they, Ivor?" Chief Inspector Slingback was getting angrier.

"In the secret room, where I left them," Ivor kept insisting.

"WELL, they're not THERE now. If Wendy doesn't get those shoes by the morning, YOU have a VERY BIG WEDGE-SHAPED problem."

"Maybe your KIDS took the SHOES!" Mr Creeper suggested.

"Why would they do that?" Ivor asked.

"YOU tell us!" Mr Creeper started to scratch all over his body.

"It's not the first time they've been in trouble, IS it?" Chief Inspector Slingback said.

"The Shoe Police told us they weren't in school. They've gone missing with the shoes," Mr Creeper told Ivor.

"That's ridiculous! They've been poorly: totally covered in SPOTS. Ask Wendy, she saw them."

Both Chief Inspector Slingback and Mr Creeper looked puzzled.

"They are VERY infectious. You don't want to go NEAR them." Ivor was saying anything he could to keep them away from Ruby and Bear.

"Nice try, Ivor. It's only a matter of time before we FIND them. And you'd better HOPE they do have those flying shoes," Mr Creeper told him.

"What kind of people are you, picking on small children? **Shoe Town** used to be a great place to live until Wendy Wedge took over. You can't trust her, she's always breaking her promises. I BET she's done that to YOU as well."

Mr Creeper and Chief Inspector Slingback looked quickly at each other. (Ivor could tell he was right.)

"We'll be back," they said in a slightly sinister way and left Ivor in a HUFF.

Left and Right were STILL sitting in front of the locker where

Bear was hiding.

"What are you doing THERE? You should be guarding Ivor,"

Mr Creeper told the dogs sternly, and pointed to the SPOT where

he wanted them to be.

They sloped over and slumped down on to the ground.

Bear held his breath until he heard the door shut behind

Mr Creeper and Chief Inspector Slingback.

DAD was SO close!

Bear just wanted to SEE him and let him know that he and

Ruby had come to RESCUE him.

But how was he going to get past

the dogs?

"SAUSAGES!" whispered Bear.

He had them in his bag.

It was worth a try.

Bear took out the leftover sausages wrapped in foil and straight away, the dogs began to growl and SNIFF the air. He opened the locker door just enough to send out the camera and check **exactly** where the dogs were.

It didn't take long to find them. The dogs could SMELL the sausages. They were getting closer and hungrier.

"Uh-oh!"

Bear THREW out the first sausage in their direction as FAR as he could.

"FETCH!"

The sausage gracefully F L E W through the air, then –

SNAP! – Right jumped up and GRABBED

it in his mouth. Next, Bear aimed for

LEFT – who, not wanting

to miss out, HURLED himself

at the sausage.

SNAP!

Then, as calmly as he could, Bear stepped out of the locker and

edged past both dogs.

"There, there. Nice doggies,"

he whispered.

Then Bear dropped a

little more sausage to give

him enough time to RESCUE Dad.

He took out his pass and scanned it,

and the door

CLICKED open.

"DAD!" Bear called out.

"Bear? What are you doing here?" Ivor said in astonishment.

"We came to rescue you!" Bear told him, and they hugged each other tightly.

"WE?" Dad repeated.

"Ruby's here too – we got separated running away from Mr Creeper and the Shoe Police."

"WHAT? Where is she?" Dad was trying to take it all in.

"She ran back the way we came. Let's go – I don't have much sausage left," Bear said, which just made Dad even more confused.

"OK – but what about the dogs?" he asked.

Bear opened the door to reveal the dogs still munching on the last bit of sausage.

"They're happy. I've only got one piece left to get us out, though," Bear said.

"Come on – what are we waiting for?" Dad smiled at Bear.

"Which way did Ruby go?"

"In the direction of Wendy's office, I think," Bear said.

"Follow me." Dad checked there was no one around before they scurried off to find Ruby.

"I NEVER know what you two are going to do next," Dad said to Bear as they ran.

"I do – we're going to win **THE GOLDEN SHOE AWARDS,"** Bear told him.

Ivor wasn't really taking anything in. He was trying not to think about what could happen if they ALL got caught.

"I hope Ruby's OK," he said as they ran down the corridor.

"Don't worry – Ruby's good at squeezing into small spaces. She'll find somewhere safe to hide,"* Bear reminded Dad.

*Foot note: Maybe, maybe not.

Hiding behind Wendy's massive desk probably wasn't the best place Ruby could have chosen. She'd *R U N* as fast as she could away from Mr Creeper and Chief Inspector Slingback and found herself right BACK where she'd started – in Wendy's office.

On the other hand, if she was QUICK, she might find a CLUE to where Dad was.

"I'm going to investigate," she thought, and crept out to look around. Everywhere she walked, the EYES of Wendy's paintings seemed to be following her – which was creepy. Ruby shivered and pulled a face, then picked up a photo of Walter as a baby and laughed.

"Ha! He's always

been a twit,"

she whispered.

"And there's Mummy twit,"
Ruby joked, looking at a picture
of Wendy. She was wearing some
zigzag-patterned wedges and,
WEIRDLY for Wendy, she was
smiling. "Chilling," Ruby muttered
and kept moving until she came to
another door. Curiosity got the better
of her and she couldn't resist having a
snoop in there too. She opened the door.

"THIS must be where Wendy lives. It's SO much bigger than our

Shoebox Estate house. Bear has to see this."

Ruby whispered into her wrist control, "Turn camera on."

Her wedge opened up and the arm stretched out, recording the

HUGE front room with W-shaped sofa and chairs and anything else

she thought looked interesting.

Next, she stepped into Wendy's bedroom. There was the

BIGGEST four-poster bed Ruby had EVER seen. (It was the only four-

poster bed she had ever seen.)

Ruby resisted the URGE to JUMP on it, but only because she

spotted a WIG. She put it on and filmed herself looking fierce.

"Can you believe Wendy wears a wig?" Ruby whispered to the

camera. "And check out the SIZE of this shoe closet."

Ruby took off the
wig and pushed
back the curtains
to reveal Wendy's
collection.

"Woah – how many pairs of wedges do you need?"* Ruby whispered.

*Footnote: turns out, quite a lot.

Inside there were rows and rows of different types of wedges, none of which looked comfortable: metal wedges with nuts and bolts holding them together, modern angular wedges, and lots of variations of Wendy's fierce-creature wedges.

Ruby couldn't resist choosing a pair to try on. She slipped her foot inside a metal wedge and balanced on one leg, putting her hand on the wall to steady herself. How can she walk in these? Ruby thought as she WOBBLED and lost her balance. She put her hand out as she fell and pushed a picture right into the wall.

"Uh-oh…"

Ruby watched as a WHOLE different cupboard suddenly sprang out. It was a secret shoe cabinet. THESE wedges looked very different to the ones on show. They looked softer, with more colours and patterns. Some had feathers and scales and all kinds of textures too.

She picked up a pair and TOUCHED the shapes on the side. They instantly changed colour.

"Wow."

There was another pair that had an interesting zigzag pattern. "Crazy," she whispered. Something told her this was a good thing to record. But as the camera took in all the WEDGES, Ruby suddenly froze. She could hear FOOTSTEPS. Heavy, thumping footsteps. The kind of footsteps that could only come from one person. "Uh-oh…"

It wasn't hard to guess WHO was about to come in.

(Take another guess…)

Thump

Thump

Thump

It WAS Wendy Wedge.

Ruby charged into the bedroom and threw herself UNDER the four-poster bed, seconds before the door SWUNG open and in marched Wendy.

Ruby could see and FEEL the HEAVY creature wedges THUMP past her.

"I'm surrounded by idiots. Just FIND the flying shoes. How hard is THAT?" Wendy was talking to herself.

She began to take off her ENORMOUS shoulder pads and put them on the stand.

The creature wedges were SO close to the edge of the bed, their sensors were picking up on Ruby and SNARLING. Ruby couldn't move a muscle.

"**If Ivor Foot hadn't been so SELFISH and just handed over the flying shoes in the first place, I wouldn't be in this position! Oh! My FEET are killing me.**"

Wendy walked past again and SAT on the bed. Ruby grimaced.

"**My aching toes,**" Wendy cried again. "**It's time for extreme measures.**"

Wendy got up to look for something and disappeared into her shoe closet. THIS was Ruby's chance to make a run for it. There wasn't much time. But as she began to roll out from under the bed ...

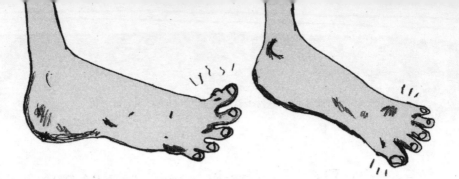

… Wendy came back, in BARE feet.

Ruby was forced to fling herself back under the bed – FAST.

Wendy walked up and down and then STOPPED. Her bony

feet were SO close to Ruby's face. Ruby held her breath (for lots

of reasons). Wendy's feet looked like they'd spent YEARS being

squeezed into very uncomfortable wedges. (Because they had.)

Ruby closed her eyes and held her breath. It was all too much.

She tucked herself as FAR back as she possibly could.

"After the DAY I've had, I need to put my FEET up and get some rest. Tomorrow's GOLDEN SHOE AWARD is going to be VERY special for me. Maybe I'll just read a few pages of my book before bed."

PHUFF

PHUFFF

Two things landed in front of Ruby.

She opened her eyes to see Wendy's gnarly old feet sliding right into…

A PAIR OF SLIPPERS
FLUFFY PINK SLIPPERS.
With POMPOMS.

Ruby put her hand over her mouth to

STOP herself from GASPING!

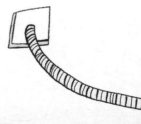

Wendy was wearing slippers. Fluffy, cosy, illegal slippers. No one would EVER believe it: the owner of World of Wedge, the MOST powerful shoe-making company in town, was in front of her right now wearing soft, comfy SLIPPERS.

Wendy sat down in a chair and got out her book. She put her slippered feet on a comfy stool and began to read. Ruby stayed perfectly still.

It was clear Ruby was going to be STUCK hiding for ages. She'd have to wait for Wendy to go to bed and fall FAST asleep before attempting to escape again.

And that could take a VERY long time.

RASSSsssssPPpPPPPPP!

RAAASSSsssssPPPPPP!

Only it didn't.

Wendy's crooked mouth dropped open and

a horrible SNOORRRrrrrrrrreee came

out in no time at all. THIS time

Ruby took her chance to LEAVE

and get to safety. She rolled out

from under the bed and began to

TIPTOE across the room. She

took a small step forward...

CREAK!

Ruby winced.

Her second step was quieter.

Third step,

fourth step...

She was nearly out. UNTIL...

294

KNOCK

KNOCK

KNOCK

Ruby FROZE like she was playing musical statues.

She turned to glance at Wendy, whose eyelids were beginning to

FLICKER. She was WAKING UP!

Ruby quickly ran behind Wendy's chair and crouched down.

"Huh? WHO'S THERE?"

Wendy mumbled and stood up.

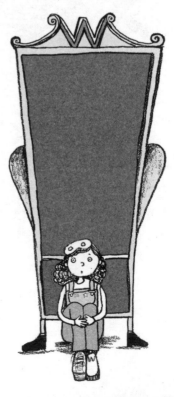

"DON'T come in!" she bellowed. **"I'll be there in a second."**

She got up and shuffled to the closet in her slippers.

"WHAT now? No peace for ME," Wendy grumbled.

KNOCK! KNOCK! KNOCK!

"I said, WAIT!" Wendy shouted. She put on her shoulder pads

and went to the door.

Ruby listened

carefully.

"Ms Wedge, I'm so

sorry to disturb you…"

"YOU should be. This

BETTER be

IMPORTANT!"

she yelled.

Ruby couldn't see who Wendy was yelling at.

"WHY DIDN'T YOU COME AND

TELL ME EARLIER? Idiots!"

Then the door closed and Ruby could make out the sound of

Wendy

STOMP
STOMP
STOMPING away.

It was NOW or never.

Ruby peeked out from behind the chair, then made a RUN for

the door, fumbled in her bag for the PASS, clicked it open and went

through…

"Uh-oh…" Ruby whispered as it closed behind her.

This didn't look right at all.

What was this place? It didn't feel like an office or part of Wendy's apartment. It was … darker. Ruby could just about make out rows of large glass tanks.

"What are those?" Ruby wondered as she edged closer to the nearest tank. The bugs inside began to flicker with tiny lights. "That's SO cool!"

She watched the mini light show, then moved on to another tank. "I'd better film THIS," Ruby whispered to herself.

Dozens of beetles were scuttling around, their gold, shiny wings flickering. Ruby went from tank to tank watching the weird, exotic-looking bugs and creatures.

"Is this some kind of zoo?" she wondered. She touched the side of a tank and the wings of the bugs rippled and pulsed with different colours.

"That's amazing," said Ruby. She did it again. The rippling movement reminded her of something, but what?

She peered into more tanks and saw bright red shiny bugs and HUGE butterflies with dazzling patterns on their wings. There was a larger cage full of tiny birds – their wings were covered with gorgeous jewel-coloured feathers.

Ruby had never seen anything like this before. There were more tanks HIGHER up that she couldn't quite see into. "I wish I was taller," she murmured, then spotted a small set of wooden steps. "Just what I need."

Ruby pulled the steps closer and climbed up to the top layer of tanks.

She still couldn't see anything. "Maybe they're empty. I'll check."

Ruby spoke into her wrist control: "Camera UP." It weaved from side to side, searching for something to film. "Camera – tap the glass," she whispered.

Tap

    Tap

        Tap

            Tap.

Still nothing. Ruby took one step back down the ladder when something moved…

… The WHOLE tank **HISSED.**

It was full of SNAKES!

SCARY, **POISONOUS,**

ZIGZAG-PATTERNED

SNAKES!

Ruby YELPED and stumbled back down the ladder.

There were SO many SNAKES. What were they doing here? This whole place was freaky and Ruby didn't like it at all.

But there was something about the snakes that looked weirdly familiar. Ruby cautiously climbed back up the ladder for another quick look.

"Where have I seen them before?" she said. She filmed them slithering around looking angry at being disturbed.

Ruby knew she had to get out of there. She climbed back down and this time she found the right door and RAN as fast

as she could …

...RIGHT into Dad!

"RUBY!" he called out.

"DAD!" she shouted.

"I'm here too!" Bear said, and

they gave each other a BIG Foot

family hug.

"Where have you been?"

Bear asked.

"You are NOT going to believe what I've just SEEN!" Ruby

said. Dad looked down at her feet.

"You're wearing the other camera shoe!"

"I've been filming, Dad. I can't wait to show you! It's going to

change everything."

"How did you even get in? Actually, don't answer that now –

we'd better get out of here." Ivor knew they didn't have much time.

"Where did you hide, Ruby?" Bear asked as they hurried after Dad.

"Loads of places – behind Wendy's desk, under her bed, behind her chair...

I saw a LOT of scary things."

"I'm not sure I want to know..."

Dad said. He still couldn't believe his kids had come to his rescue. They were as brave and as brilliant as their mum – she would have been so proud of them.

Ruby and Bear followed Dad out of the WOW building and back to Betty's house as quickly as they could. Dad knew his ESCAPE would make Wendy even more **FURIOUS.** She'd go **BALLISTIC** with **ANGER.** He could imagine her face.

Ivor smiled. His kids were the best.

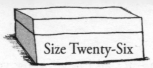

Size Twenty-Six

The sun was coming up when Chelsea knocked on her mum's bedroom door, holding a cup of tea.

"Thank you, Chelsea – that's nice of you. What have you broken?" Betty asked, only half joking.

"Nothing." Chelsea smiled. "Someone's here. I thought I'd come and tell you."

"WHO? Not Wendy Wedge!" Betty put down her cup of tea.

"No – you would have heard HER coming a MILE off. It's a surprise!"

The last person Betty was expecting to see was Ivor. "Are you OK?" How on earth did you escape Wendy's clutches?" Betty asked.

"It's all thanks to these SUPERHERO children. They got me out," Ivor told Betty, who was stunned.

"Don't worry, Mum – it's all fine. We put your WOW pass back," Chelsea explained.

"You used my pass?!" Betty asked. "What about the security cameras?"

"We had masks and balloons," Ruby explained.

"Don't think about it now, Betty. We need to work out WHAT to do next. Wendy's not going to give up looking for us," Ivor told her.

"You're right – the shoe police will be out in force. In case anyone's forgotten, it's **THE GOLDEN SHOE AWARDS** today. And I've got to go to work and pretend that EVERYTHING'S fine. Which isn't going to be easy," Betty said.

"At least Mr Creeper didn't find the flying shoes. That's something. Speaking of which, where can they be?" Ivor said. "I wonder whether they're still in the house."

"No," said Ruby and Bear, answering at the same time.

"SO, let me get this right. Wendy doesn't have flying shoes.

Mr Creeper doesn't have them, and they're NOT at our house.

WHO has them, then?"

Ivor put his head in his hands.

"Well, BERT is trying to make a new pair," Betty said, which

didn't make any sense to Ivor at all.

"He's using the special book of Mum's that I found. Bert's going

to make the flying shoes and WIN

THE GOLDEN SHOE AWARD

for YOU and MUM," Ruby told Dad happily.

"Bert's the only shoemaker who hasn't signed

Wendy's terrible contract. He's been up all night working on them,"

Betty tried to explain to Ivor, whose head was spinning now.

"But if we can't find the flying shoes, Wendy will put me in prison.

For owning slippers. Which weren't even mine!"

Ruby JUMPED up.

That's it! Slippers! I knew there was something I wanted to tell you!"

"What is it?" Dad asked, when suddenly there was a knock on the door.

"Who's that?" Betty asked suspiciously, and peeked out of the window to see three shoe officers standing there.

"You all go and HIDE. We'll deal with it, won't we, Chelsea?" said Betty.

"Leave it to me, Mum… I've got this," said Chelsea and she went to answer the door.

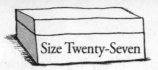

There were three police officers

outside and one (hungry-looking) small dog.

"Is your mum here?" Officer Sneaker asked

Chelsea. She gave the officers a sweet smile.

"Yes," said Chelsea. "Do you want to speak to her?"

"Yes. We need to come in and search your house,"

Officer Scarpin said.

"Are you allowed to do that?" Chelsea asked.

"Yes," Officer Trainer told her, frowning.

"Who says?"

"Eeeeerrr, Wendy Wedge, that's WHO."

"But what if I don't want to let you in?"

The police were puzzled.

"You have to," Officer Trainer told her.

"No, I don't – what's the password?" Chelsea asked.

"This isn't a game," said Officer Scarpin.

"Password, please, and I'll let you in."

The officers talked amongst themselves and then turned back.

"OK – is it SHOES...?"

"Nope. Try again."

"WEDGES?"

"NO!"

"LOOK, kid, we don't

have all day. Just let us in."

"You have to say the password," Chelsea said firmly. She was

really, really enjoying herself.

"We're coming in, ready or not," Officer Trainer said.

"The password's PLEASE. You should really learn to be more polite," Chelsea huffed, then called out, "MUM!"

Betty was cooking sausages in the kitchen and the smell was already wafting through the house, making the dog's nose twitch.

"What can I do for you, officers?" Betty asked.

"We're here to search your house," Officer Sneaker repeated.

"Why?"

"We're looking for flying shoes and anyone from the notorious Foot family. Do you know anything about these shoes or, um, Foot folk?"

"Not really," Betty said calmly. "But feel free to look around."

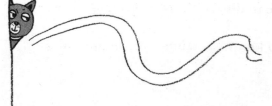

She could see the officers were

distracted by the smell of

food. "Would you officers

like a sausage sandwich?"

she asked.

"Maybe one for the dog, too?"

The officers hesitated.

"We're on duty," Officer Trainer reminded the others.

"We're due a break," Officer Scarpin whispered. "Quick look round

and then have something to eat?"

"I AM starving," Officer Trainer said.

"And it's going to be a long day, with the awards tonight,"

Officer Sneaker added.

They had a short huddle to discuss the options, then Officer

Trainer asked, "We need to know something very important first…"

"Go on."

"Do you have any ketchup?"

"Of course," Betty assured them.

"And I'm vegetarian," Officer Scarpin told Betty.

"I have veggie bacon. I'll do some for you."

Then Officer Sneaker put up his hand.

"I'm gluten free."

"No problem. I've got special bread."

"Vegan?" Officer Trainer added.

"Yup, got that covered too."

Betty had all the answers.

"Right, that's settled then. We'll stay."

The officers took the quickest of glances into every room, easily missing the Foot family hiding in the bath. Which was JUST what Betty had wanted.

All Clear

The officers happily tucked into breakfast and enjoyed every last mouthful. "Lovely to meet you both. We'll remember the password next time, Chelsea!" said Officer Trainer with a laugh.

"See you at the awards!" Officer Scarpin said.

"Yes, see you there!" Betty waved goodbye.

As soon as they'd gone, Betty went to tell Ivor and the kids it was safe to come out. She found them in Chelsea's room – fast asleep. *They must be exhausted*, Betty thought, and left them to get some rest.

BERT had been working all night too, and NO NEWS wasn't going to be GOOD NEWS, Betty decided. "Poor Bert. Making flying shoes in SUCH a short time is an impossible task. It will be a SHOE miracle if he's succeeded."

"WHHOPPPEEEE!"

Size Twenty-Eight

BERT had only gone and DONE IT!

He'd followed all Sally's instructions and made the flying shoes!

Now he was busy testing them out, and so far the shoes were

working a **treat**. Bert couldn't stop LAUGHING and smiling as

he zoomed around the room.

"THESE ARE THE BEST SHOES EVER! WE'RE GOING TO WIN **THE GOLDEN SHOE AWARD** NOW!"

Bert cheered.

He was so busy making so much noise that he didn't hear the

shop door being KICKED open or the PING that meant someone

had come in. And he missed the **THUD THUD THUD** of VERY

heavy footsteps until it was too late…

"GIVE ME THOSE FLYING SHOES!"

a voice bellowed from the ground.

It was Wendy Wedge with Mr Creeper. Bert hovered in the air.

"No, I will not. Get out of MY SHOP!" Bert said, still flying above their heads.

"THEY'RE MY SHOES now. COME DOWN, or things could get NASTY," Wendy ordered.

"No," Bert shot back.

"You will, OR ELSE." Wendy wasn't used to anyone disobeying her.

"I won't!" Bert shouted.

"You will!"

"I won't."

"YOU WILL TOO! GET them, Mr Creeper – RIP them from his feet!" Wendy demanded. Bert tucked his legs up tightly. Mr Creeper was tall – but not THAT tall.

"STAY AWAY! I'm not coming DOWN!" Bert told

them, but the shoes' inbuilt voice control heard Bert

say "DOWN" and that's what they did. Bert floated

towards the ground, just enough for Mr Creeper

to grab one of his ankles and drag the shoes OFF

his feet one by one. Bert dropped to the floor

with a THUMP.

"Bert, are you OK?" Wendy asked, stepping

OVER him to take the shoes.

"You don't care – all you care about is yourself,"

Bert said angrily.

"You know me so well." Wendy laughed.

Bert was FURIOUS. He sat there in a crumpled heap and told

Wendy exactly what he thought of her.

"YOU'RE a MEAN, spiteful, TERRIBLE person."

"Thank you. I try my best."

"It's not a compliment," Bert snapped through gritted teeth.

Things were about to get EVEN WORSE

for Bert. Mr Creeper spotted Sally's book.

"Ms Wedge, THIS is the book Bert dropped. All the instructions

for making flying shoes are in HERE." Mr Creeper handed the book

to Wendy. The promotion was his now. He could feel it.

"HOW very useful." Wendy flicked through a few pages, then

dropped it in her OVERSIZED bag.

 "NO! You can't take that. It's Ivor's!"

Bert shouted at them.

"What's Ivor's is MINE," Wendy said smugly. **"It's a**

shoeTASTIC BOOK and I'm going to enjoy using it. We would

stay longer, Bert, but I have an important GOLDEN SHOE

AWARD to win with these FLYING SHOES!" Wendy laughed,

which sounded like a MOOSE coughing.

"Ha! Ha! Ha! Ha!

Harrrrr Harrrrr!"

"And, Bert? Enjoy your little shop – you won't have it for much longer. But don't worry, you can always come and work for ME. Everyone does in the end."

Wendy smiled then flicked a few of his lovely brogues on to the floor as she stomped out of the shop.

Bert groaned. All that hard work – for NOTHING!

Bert was SO angry.

It was WORSE than nothing...

It was all for WENDY WEDGE.

He'd had the flying shoes ON HIS FEET.

What was he going to tell Betty and the kids now?

The truth: that Wendy was a ROTTEN, GHASTLY, SELFISH, FIENDISH, SNEAKY, STOMPY, GRUMPY, THUMPY, HIDEOUS, NO GOOD, MEAN, WEDGEAWFUL* PERSON.

And anything else he could think of.

*Footnote: He might have made that one up – but you get the idea.

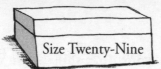

Size Twenty-Nine

DING-DONG

The doorbell was ringing.

"NOT the police back again, surely?" Betty peeked out of the window. It wasn't the police. It was Bert, and from the look on his face he didn't have good news. Betty let him in straight away and said, "Bert, don't worry, you did your best. It was a lot to expect. I'm sorry the shoes didn't work."

She was trying her hardest to make him feel better.

"Oh, but they DID work!" Bert wailed as he walked in. "They worked perfectly. Then SHE of the WEDGE foot barged in with her horrible SIDEKICK and STOLE them and Sally's book too. It's a DISASTER!" Bert took a breath.

Just then, Chelsea ran in. "Ivor, Ruby and Bear are

awake!" she said

"Ivor's HERE?" Bert asked.

"I sure am," Ivor said, walking into the kitchen.

He yawned and stretched.

"These fantastic children helped me escape!

We've been hiding – I must have fallen asleep.

I feel so much better now."

"Well, I'm sorry, Ivor, but THAT's not going

to last long. I made flying shoes last night. But Wendy Wedge stole

them AND Sally's book.

"Wendy's got Mum's BOOK?" Ruby asked.

"I'm so sorry. They just TOOK it from me. We have to do

something. She can't get away with it."

Bert was devastated.

(No one was happy with the Wendy Wedge situation.)

"If Wendy wins **THE GOLDEN SHOE AWARD** she'll take over all the other towns and cities too. With her BIG clumpy wedges that have no SOUL," Ivor told them.

Bert nodded. "I'll lose my shop for sure. We need a plan."

The three of them carried on discussing what a terrible business this all was and no one seemed to know what to do next. It was almost like Wendy had WON already.

"Hey, Ruby – remember you promised to tell me what you saw in Wendy's office? Now's a good time," said Bear. Ruby jumped UP and began to do star jumps.

"Ruby, what are you doing?" Bear asked crossly.

"I'm just EXCITED!" said Ruby, jumping faster. "You won't

believe it."

"Ruby, sit down. You're making everything wobble," Dad told her.

"Sorry, Ruby – please stop. I can't THINK if you

JUMP." Bert had his head in his hands.

"When I show you what I saw, Bert,

you'll be jumping for joy too."

"I doubt that." Bert wasn't in a jumping mood.

"OK, Ruby, we're listening," Dad said.

Ruby danced over to her bag and pulled out the camera wedge.

Ruby SET it to PLAYBACK. "Remember when I told you I HID under Wendy's bed?"

"Yes, though I'm trying not to think about it," Dad told her.

"The WHOLE of **Shoe Town** needs to SEE what kind of a person Wendy Wedge really is and what she's been up to," Ruby told them impressively.

"YES, Ruby," Bear chipped in. "Get on with it."

"Today everyone will be at **THE GOLDEN SHOE AWARDS.** And THAT'S where we HAVE to show THIS."

The film started and they all watched it OPEN-MOUTHED.

Dad broke into a BIG smile. Betty BEAMED. Chelsea grinned. Bear gave Ruby a high five.

"I'm ready to do some star jumps, if that's OK," Bert said.

Finally, it looked like they might be able to DO something about Wendy Wedge. No one was going to prison, and from the LOOKS on everyone's faces, things were going to change for the BETTER.

(At least, that's what they all HOPED.)

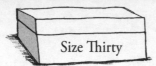

Size Thirty

"THIS IS BRILLIANT!

This is EVIDENCE that Wendy has

been up to NO good. She won't have a

WEDGE to stand on," Dad told them,

cheering with relief. He had watched Ruby's

film ten times now and every time it got better.

Ruby and Chelsea had kicked off their wedges and were

dancing. Ruby called it "the SHOE shuffle".

Bert was still doing star jumps.

Betty cleared her throat. "Sorry to break up the party – I need to go. I'll be backstage at **THE GOLDEN SHOE AWARDS,** so wait for my signal to come to the main CONTROL room. Ivor – you bring the camera. Bert – you keep a lookout. Ruby, Bear, Chelsea – YOU guys need to cause a distraction to keep the shoe police away. Your DANCE would be perfect, or something DRAMATIC. Right. Is everyone READY?" Betty wanted to CHECK that EVERYONE was clear about the PLAN.

"We need a code name," said Bear.

"This is like a military operation," Bert agreed.

"How about operation WEDGE?" Ivor suggested.

"WEDGE WARS!" Chelsea shouted.

"Wendy has too many things named after her already," said Ruby. "We've got a name already – SHOE WARS?" she suggested.

"Nice!" Bert smiled.

"SHOE WARS it is, then," Betty said.

They all did a PINKY PROMISE to STOP

the DREADED WENDY WEDGE

from EVER winning

THE GOLDEN SHOE AWARD

with FLYING SHOES.

(Shoo was excited to see the back of Wendy Wedge, too.)

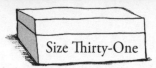

Size Thirty-One

Wendy was in a SUPER-good mood that morning, with the flying shoes finally in her greedy grasp and **THE GOLDEN SHOE AWARDS** just hours later.

Paying an early visit to see Bert had been a GOOD move on her part. NOW she had a REAL pair of flying shoes. And they were FANTASTIC – just like she'd always dreamed they would be.

Wendy had tried them out around the apartment already and she was looking forward to **THE GOLDEN SHOE AWARDS** EVEN MORE. Just thinking about it was making her feel all tingly. There was a knock at the door and Wendy shouted, **"ENTER."**

Mr Creeper shuffled in.

"Is THAT what you're wearing for the awards? I hope not,"

was the first thing Wendy said to him.

"It's a new tie," Mr Creeper told her.

"Did you keep the receipt?"

Wendy asked, not even joking.

"Was that why you wanted to see me, Ms Wedge?" he asked.

"No. I wanted to tell you something exciting."

Mr Creeper stood up taller. This was it, this was the

promotion he'd been waiting for. Not even Ivor Foot's mysterious

disappearance was going to SPOIL his day.

"THINGS are going to be CHANGING around here," Wendy

told him. **"Everyone will want to own a pair of flying shoes, so**

production and security has got to be STEPPED UP."

"Yes, Ms Wedge," he agreed.

"So," Wendy continued, a mean smile forming on her lips. **"I'd**

like you to meet my NEW head of security."

"I'm sorry?" Mr Creeper thought he'd misheard.

A stern-looking woman with a pinched mouth and mean eyes stomped in.

"Ms Hobnail will be taking control of a lot of things here at WOW, including the development of the new range of flying wedges and ALL the security too. She's VERY experienced."

"Thank you, Ms Wedge," she replied.

"But, but … that's MY job, Ms Wedge," Mr Creeper stammered.

"WAS your job. I've got plenty of other … things for you to do. Walter needs some training up. Otherwise, HOW will he ever take over the family empire one day?"

Mr Creeper didn't like the sound of this.

"It's a new era at WOW," Wendy continued.

"We'll need to start bringing in machines to make the flying shoes and get rid of a few miserable people."

She stared at Mr Creeper.

"But half the TOWN works here," Mr Creeper reminded her.

"EXACTLY! Think of the money I'll save!"

Ms Hobnail interrupted them. "Ms Wedge, I have that security footage you requested."

"Excellent. Mr Creeper, FEAST your eyes on this."

 She clicked a remote. A video started to play of WOW the night before.

Mr Creeper watched in horror as the Foot children sneaked out of the building with their dad.

"Oh dear, my head of security fooled by children in masks with sausages. Very POOR, don't you think, Mr Creeper?" Wendy snarled.

It wouldn't have happened on my watch," Ms Hobnail said.

"AND I had to find the shoes MYSELF!" Wendy grimaced.

"All this time, Ivor was lying to me, AND those children are a PAIN.

Those dogs are refusing to eat anything else BUT sausages now, HOPELESS. Plus, promotions need to be EARNED, Mr Creeper. For doing something EXTRA – and you failed to find the shoes. You're lucky Ms Hobnail will be fixing your mistakes and overseeing **THE GOLDEN SHOE AWARDS** ceremony."

Mr Creeper was defeated. "Just tell me what you need, Ms Wedge," he said quietly.

"Excellent, that's what I like to hear. You can bring Walter down to my dressing room. Thank you, Mr Creeper. Let's not be SHOE-PID about this."

Wendy dismissed Mr Creeper with a wave of her hand,

and then turned to her NEW head of security.

"Now, Ms Hobnail, we need to go through the DETAILS for

tonight. I want EVERYTHING to be perfect."

Mr Creeper slumped out of Wendy's office to find Walter was

already there waiting (and tapping his foot).

"You took your time," Walter told Mr Creeper rudely.

"Your mother wants you to wait in her dressing room. Let's go," he said wearily.

"That's boring. I have a better idea. YOU'RE always going into THAT room. WHAT'S in there? I want to know," Walter said, pointing at the door which led to Wendy's secret room full of creatures.

"You're not allowed to know or go in there. Your mother said so. It's locked," Mr Creeper replied.

"RUBBISH. I can do what I want," Walter said, then snatched Mr Creeper's pass and PUSHED past him.

Mr Creeper wasn't in the mood to argue. He knew Walter

REALLY didn't like snakes. It was one of many reasons Wendy kept

the door locked and it would serve him right to have a scare.

Mr Creeper decided to just wait for Walter to come out…

… which

didn't take

very long.

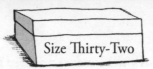

Betty left her house and set off for the WOW building. She'd present her MUSIC wedges at **THE GOLDEN SHOE AWARDS** just like she was supposed to, and try to PRETEND that everything was fine.

Wendy Wedge couldn't suspect a thing – and that wasn't going to be easy.

Betty was already feeling a little nervous. So the last thing she needed was anyone asking her difficult questions, like the Shoe Police or Mrs Court ... who suddenly SPRANG out of nowhere.

"Ms Boot, I'm glad I caught you," she said.

"I'm in a bit of a hurry. I can't stop, Mrs Court. I've got a lot on. It's **THE GOLDEN SHOE AWARDS** today," Betty reminded her.

340

"Haven't we all, Ms Boot? I wanted to say good luck," Mrs Court replied.

"Oh, thank you. Yes, I'll need it," Betty said, surprised.

"I'm assuming the Foot family are going too?" Mrs Court asked.

"Errr … maybe. I'm not really sure," said Betty vaguely.

"I think you DO know, Ms Boot," Mrs Court said, and gave her a look. Then she TWISTED the handle of her walking stick, clicked it in half, pulled out two flaps, pushed a few buttons, snapped out some tiny wheels, and the whole stick became a mini scooter. Mrs Court ZOOMED OFF down the road.

"Bye, Mrs Court. See you at the AWARDS?" Betty

called after her.

"YOU most certainly will!"

she called back.

The HUGE W building of Wedge Footquarters was lit up against the night sky. It looked SPECTACULAR. People from towns and cities all over were arriving for **THE GOLDEN SHOE AWARDS.**

TV presenters Kelly Kitten and Peter Peeptoe were broadcasting LIVE from the purple carpet. Their show, "SHOE TIME", could be seen on HUGE screens all around the World of Wedge venue.

"So the BIG question everyone is asking is: will Shoehampton hold on to their record for the MOST **GOLDEN SHOE AWARD** wins ever? Or will rival cities Big Toehampton or Little Toehampton take the title? What do you think, Pete?"

"It's hard to call it right now, Kelly. Don't forget about the NEWcomers Stepford Town, and last year's second-place holders, Walking-On-Sea. Those "Walk on Water" shoes they showed in the regional semi-finals were shoeTASTIC – don't you agree, Kelly?"

Kelly Kitten walked around the stage smiling and talking to the camera.

"Then there's Sneakerville, the city that's been quietly climbing the SHOE ladder. But THIS year is all about **Shoe Town."**

"You mean WEDGE Town, Kelly. Wendy Wedge changed the name," Pete corrected.

"Of course she did. Everyone's wondering just WHAT Wendy Wedge at World of Wedge will be bringing to the party this time? If she gets it right, Pete, she could be on the WEDGE OF GLORY!"

"I'm resisting the URGE to sing, Kelly."

"Good job, Pete. And now let's go to a commercial break."

The whole of **Shoe Town** was buzzing with excitement about that evening's awards ceremony. Wendy Wedge had arrived in her private dressing room to get a little "quiet time" before her BIG AWARD moment.

Walter was already there and getting over his snake SHOCK by doing what HE thought was excellent tap dancing. This wasn't helping Wendy's stress levels.

After ten minutes (it felt like longer) Wendy asked him to stop.

"Walter, be a dear and do literally ANYTHING ELSE, will you?"

"But these tap shoes I found are fun," he told her.

"Not for me, they're not."

Walter frowned, folded his arms and sulked.

"Walter, dearest, you have to understand this is a very special time. I will be forever remembered not just for WINNING

THE GOLDEN SHOE AWARD, but for winning with

never-before-seen flying shoes. I think this will be the VERY

BEST moment of my ENTIRE LIFE!" Wendy sighed happily.

"Apart from when I was born," Walter added.

"That goes without saying." Wendy smiled

(without actually saying it).

"You look very smart, Walter," she told him so

he'd stop sulking.

"What are these?" Walter asked, moving

on to the ELABORATE table of food.

"CHOUX buns. Help

yourself – oh, you

already have."

Manners weren't

a strong point for Walter (or Wendy).

Walter took a plate of food then flopped on to the HUGE sofa.

He turned on the W I D E screen TV to see that "SHOE TIME"

was coming live from outside the WOW building. A picture of

Wendy appeared on screen.

"LOOK, Mother. They're talking about you," Walter told her.

"Of COURSE they are – I'm very important. Let me listen."

Wendy turned the sound UP.

"And we're BACK at this year's **GOLDEN SHOE**

AWARD, where the BEST **shoe towns** and cities will BATTLE

it out to be crowned the WINNER! Wendy Wedge – and WEDGE

TOWN – are hoping this is their year. What do you think, Kelly?

Will WOW wow the judges?"

"Of course I will!"

Wendy shouted at the TV.

"Not sure, Pete. Wedge footwear can be a little bit on the STODGY side. A bit CLUMPY, LUMPY, sometimes even THUMPY. I mean, YOU KNOW when Wendy Wedge is on the approach, right?"

"Ha! Yes, Kelly, she makes an IMPACT, that's for sure!"

At this point Wendy turned the sound OFF.

"Awwww, I was watching that!" Walter complained.

"They're FOOLS! What do THEY know about fabulous FOOTWEAR? NOTHING! That's what. I'll show THEM and anyone who EVER doubted me," Wendy sneered.

Walter kept watching the silent television screen. As the camera panned over the huge crowd of people arriving, he shuffled closer to the TV and peered more closely at the screen. "Mother, LOOK! it's the Foot Family and Bert Brogue in some ... WEIRD disguises. I can spot them a mile off."

Wendy came over and squinted at the screen.

"Oh, yes! SO it is! How nice of them to come as a group. It will be so much easier to arrest them ALL TOGETHER. I'll let the NEW guards know where to find them – RIGHT NOW. VERY good job, Walter." Wendy rubbed her hands together in anticipation.

"Thank you, Mother. I might do another quick tap dance." Walter smiled.

"Absolutely NOT," Wendy told him swiftly.

There was a knock at the door. It was Officer T-Bar coming to

tell Wendy the awards were about to begin.

**"THIS is MY MOMENT
to SOAR. I am ready
for my CLOSE-UP,"**

Wendy said dramatically.

She stood in front of the mirror to check her pose and practise

her winner's speech. She didn't need to remember a list of names,

because she wasn't planning on thanking anyone.

Walter crammed more food into his mouth and tap-danced

behind his mother as she THUMPED her way backstage.

Tap, tap, tap, tappety-tap…

THUMP.

THUMP.

THUMP.

THUMP.

(Everybody could tell that

Wendy was on her way.)

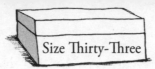

"Do you think anyone will recognize us?" Ruby whispered to Bear.

"I don't think so," Bear said and slipped in his fake teeth.

"They suit you!" Ruby laughed.

"Can you talk properly?" Chelsea asked.

"Naw wearly," Bear tried.

"Even better." Ruby smiled and flicked back her long black Halloween-witch's wig. Along with the fake teeth, Bear wore a floppy hat, Chelsea had on STAR glasses and a cape. Bert's fake moustache and spiky wig were a triumph of disguise. And Ivor's curly wig looked almost real.

They joined the queue to go in. A guard that Ivor didn't

recognize stopped them. He spoke to Bear.

"How old are you? No kids allowed in on their own."

Bear shook his head. He couldn't talk or else his teeth would fall

out.

"They're all with me," Ivor said as confidently as he could.

"OK. Do you know where you're going?" the guard asked Bear,

who opened his mouth to answer. The guard looked horrified as the

teeth dropped into his hand.

"Oops!"

There were signs EVERYWHERE that said:

NO PHONES OR CAMERAS – OR ELSE!

Ivor had snuck in two cameras – by wearing them! It was a HUGE relief that he hadn't been stopped. Now they were safely inside the grounds of WOW, Ivor took them off – he was just in his socks, but that didn't matter. He gave one of the camera wedges to Ruby and Bear to hold.

"Put on the wrist control and we can keep in touch," he told them. "Now you guys head to the front and keep a look-out for Betty's signal."

"We'll head to the control room, and once YOU give us the all-clear, then it's SHOE WARS all the way," Bert reminded everyone. "Ruby, why are you laughing?"

"Sorry," Ruby giggled. "It's just your moustache. It looks really funny."

Ivor and Bert headed to the control room while Ruby, Bear and Chelsea mingled with the crowds, trying not to stick out – but failing.

None of this went unnoticed by Ms Hobnail and her NEW

security team. They had already ZOOMED in on the odd

collection of people.

"Focus on that lot…" she said. "They're UP to something. They

could be the Foot gang Ms Wedge is looking for."

"Shall we arrest them now?" Security Officer Plimsoll asked.

"Not yet – let's keep watching. Ms Wedge wants to wait for the

right moment," Ms Hobnail said in a very threatening way.

Meanwhile, Betty had a PROBLEM.

Her pass had stopped working and the control room was now
surrounded by NEW security guards. It was going to be impossible
to get in and Betty HAD to warn Ivor and Bert. Finding another
way to get their film on the big screen wasn't going to be easy.
Backstage, Betty paced around her co-workers, wondering what to
do next. Ms Hobnail appeared. "There's been a change of plan. You
lot aren't needed any more – apart from YOU, Betty Boot. You stay
RIGHT here."

"WHY me?" Betty asked.

"Just do as I say…"

Ms Hobnail told her.

She was in a right mood.

"But who's going to represent Shoe— I mean, WEDGE

TOWN? We've ALL worked so hard on these SHOW-STOPPING

wedges," Phillip Flop told Ms Hobnail. (like she cared)

"STUPID question – Wendy Wedge, of COURSE. She's

confident of a win and you lot will just make things more

complicated. Betty Boot, don't move a muscle," Ms Hobnail

snarled, then gestured to the security guards to keep an EYE on her.

Betty didn't like the way things were going. She waited until

Ms Hobnail had left before edging her way to the side of the stage.

"Exciting!" Betty said, trying to assure the guards that she was

just being curious. Then she peeked around the BIG screen to see

a HUGE crowd of expectant people who were all waiting for the

awards to begin. Thanks to their choice of disguises, Betty spotted

Ruby, Bear and Chelsea straight away. (They weren't exactly blending in.)

Betty waved furiously, trying to attract their attention.

"Look, there's Betty." Bear waved back.

THE GOLDEN
SHOE AWARD

"That's the signal," Chelsea said. Ruby turned on her wrist control.

"Ivor and Bert, Shoe Wars is GO."

The lights went down and spotlights circled the WHOLE venue.

A pulsating piece of music began, and the crowd went quiet, apart

from one person who couldn't stop coughing (there's always one).

The lights picked out each judge as they were introduced.

They waved to the audience as they CHEERED. Lastly, the

camera went on to…

THE GOLDEN SHOE AWARD.

There was a BIG GASP and the audience clapped some more.

The award was a stylish GOLD shoe on a stand under a glass dome.

The announcer boomed,

"So, now you've met the judges, let's get on with the awards. I've

just been told there's a small change to the schedule…"

"... WEDGE TOWN will be represented

EXCLUSIVELY by ... the one and ONLY

Wendy Wedge!"

There was a light ripple of applause.

(But not much. Wendy was not very popular.)

"Sit back and enjoy the spectacle that is

THE GOLDEN SHOE AWARDS!"

Flashing lights and roving spotlights hit the shoewalk and the

award began to GLOW.

"INTRODUCING OUR FIRST CONTESTANT

FROM SHOECASTLE.

THIS YEAR THEY BRING YOU

THE SUSHI SHOE –

A REVOLVING CONVEYOR

BELT OF TASTY TREATS

CONTAINED IN A COOL

ENVIRONMENT.

STYLISH FOOD

FOR YOUR FEET."

Next up: THE SHOE GARDEN.

A FEAST FOR THE EYES, SUPER GOOD FOR THE
ENVIRONMENT, AND COMPLETE WITH BUILT-IN
WATERING SYSTEM. IT REGROWS EVERY FEW WEEKS.
IT'S A REALLY LEAF-TASTIC SHOE."

367

"THERE'S NOTHING SMALL ABOUT

THESE TENNIS SHOES FROM

LITTLE TOEHAMPTON –

THEY AUTOMATICALLY MOVE TO WHERE THE BALL IS,

AND THE GRAB-HANDS MEAN NEVER HAVING TO PICK

UP A BALL AGAIN, EVER!

AND HERE COME THE EXTRA-SPEEDY, SOUPED-UP CAR

SHOES WITH

HOT WHEELS! I hope they're

SUPPOSED to be on fire!"

"YOU'LL NEVER WANT TO TAKE

OFF THESE BOOK SHOES FROM
BIG TOEHAMPTON,

WITH ADDED READING LIGHT AND AUTOMATIC

PAGE-TURNING TOO."

So far the display of shoes looked EXCITING. The judges were

feverishly writing and scoring each shoe. There were cries of

"Oooooooooooh" for **SNEAKERVILLE'S** endless waterfall shoes…

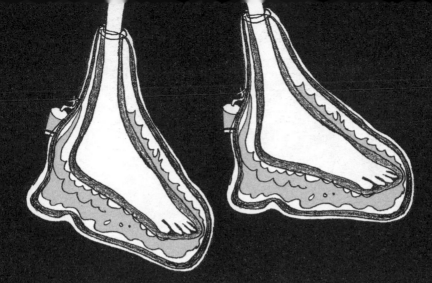

"THE SHOES THAT COOL YOUR FEET! YOU'LL ALWAYS

HAVE WATER ON TAP."

Then there were "AHHHHHHHHs" when the HOVER

SHOES floated down the shoewalk –

until they **BURST**

and deflated.

(Deflating the judges too.)

The rechargeable PHONE shoes were a bit underwhelming.

But everyone loved the chameleon shoes.

The OCTI shoes STUCK to the sides of the WALL in an excellent demonstration of SUCTION power.

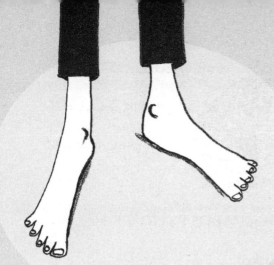

(The invisible shoes fooled NO ONE.)

With the awards in FULL FLOW, Ivor and Bert made their way to the control room. "Uh-oh, this isn't going to work," Ivor whispered.

There were GUARDS EVERYWHERE.

"What's plan B then?" Bert asked.

Ivor thought for a moment. "Storm the stage?"

Bert looked shocked. "Really?"

"OK, maybe not. We could CUT the power and project the film directly from the CAMERA SHOE on to the big screen," Ivor said. "Just like Ruby suggested."

Bert agreed and plan B it was.

Setting off to locate the central FUSE box backstage, Bert and Ivor tried their BEST to keep a low profile. All the time, Ms Hobnail and the security team were still following them with their cameras – VERY closely.

"I've seen enough – arrest them!" she announced to ALL her security officers.

Ms Hobnail checked the time – Wendy Wedge was due to be going on the SHOEWALK very soon. Ms Hobnail was pleased that everything was under control.

"Ms Hobnail." One eagle-eyed security guard got her attention. "We've detected unusual activity in the WOW building and it's heading straight towards **THE GOLDEN SHOE AWARDS** – at GREAT SPEED."

"Let me take a look." Ms Hobnail ordered them to zoom in and FREEZE-FRAMED several of the cameras.

"Is that what I think it is?" a security guard asked in a slightly ALARMED way.

"YES, I think it is. WE ALL need to stay CALM! I've GOT this," Ms Hobnail shouted, while NOT sounding very calm at all.

Bert moved into position to TURN off the power while Ivor hid by the side of the stage. He was POISED to LEAP into ACTION and show EVERYONE what a MASSIVE LIAR Wendy Wedge was.

Bert opened the grey box and put his hands on the red lever, ready to turn OFF the power…

When a voice behind him said, "Don't MOVE a MUSCLE."

Bert froze – he'd been CAUGHT red-handed.

"Look at your FEET," the voice said, and this time Bert recognized who it was.

"Betty?" said Bert, then he glanced downwards.

SNAKES!

Bert stayed as still as he could. "OH NO!"

It was FAR too dangerous to turn off the power now.

"Stay calm – everything will be fine. They'll be gone soon," Betty told him as one after the other, the snakes slithered across his feet.

Betty was right, the snakes soon slithered off. But it was too late. "Hold it right there," came a cold voice. It was one of Ms Hobnail's guards "You are ALL under arrest."

Hisssssssssss

While Bert was FOOT deep in poisonous snakes, back with
"SHOE TIME" the camera had cut to Kelly Kitten and Peter
Peeptoe, who were BEAMED on to the BIG screen. It was clear
they had been told to fill in the time.

"Hello, looks like there's a little delay before we can get to see
anything else. Isn't that right, Pete?"

"We've seen some SUPERB shoes, haven't we, Kelly?"

"Yes we have, Pete. I wonder if they'd look as good on my size seven feet?"

"Wow, that's bigger than I thought they were, Kelly."

"What's wrong with being a size seven, Pete?"

"Nothing at all. We're STILL looking for the shoe that's really going to KNOCK our socks off, right, Kelly?"

"Seven is a normal foot size – I'm just saying. I mean, WHAT size are you?"

"I think we're going to another BREAK... Back in five," Pete said.

"Seven is a good size," Kelly muttered.

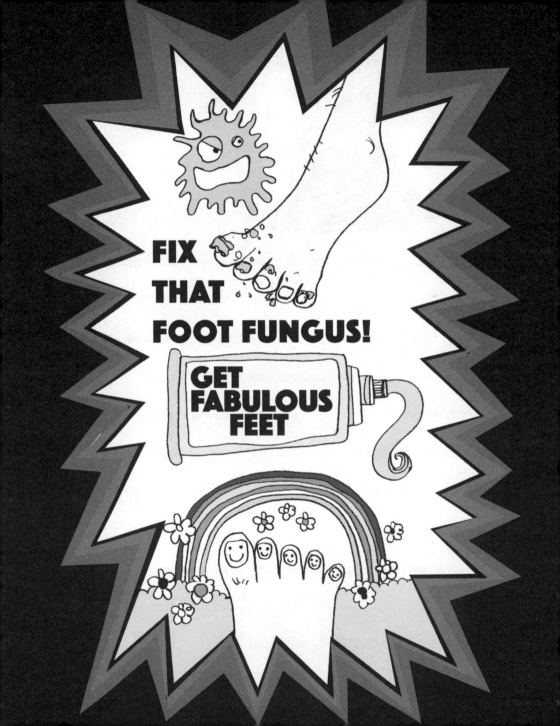

Meanwhile Wendy had put on her flying shoes and was ready to make her grand **ENTRANCE.** The one she'd DREAMED about for so many years!

She waited…   And waited…

BUT there was some kind of HOLD-up.

"What's going ON?"

Wendy demanded. **"Why is it taking so long?"**

Mr Creeper was standing next to her and he shrugged his shoulders. "You'd better ask your NEW head of security. Here she comes now."

Ms Hobnail waddled over to see them. She looked serious.

"Ms Hobnail, there BETTER be a good reason for this DELAY."

"Ms Wedge, there is. We have a VERY BIG problem."

"I AGREE – I SHOULD be holding the award by now. Let's get started, shall we?"

"We can't, Ms Wedge. I'm afraid we might have to EVACUATE and ABANDON the whole award show for safety reasons," she told Wendy.

"WHAT ARE YOU TALKING ABOUT? Don't be ridiculous. Mr Creeper, tell her – I'm not leaving."

Mr Creeper hesitated. "Ms Wedge, maybe you should listen…"

"I'M NOT GOING ANYWHERE –

just sort out the problem. I've got an award to WIN!" Wendy shouted at them, and prepared herself to walk on stage.

Ms Hobnail tried again. "Ms Wedge, our security cameras have spotted LOTS of RARE, POISONOUS SNAKES on the loose. We've found some backstage. The rest could be anywhere. We don't want the situation to get out of control."

Wendy ROLLED her eyes.

"ARE you kidding me? WHAT KIND OF FOOL LET THOSE SNAKES OUT in the FIRST place? They're only a tiny bit poisonous, by the way. Who's the IDIOT who WASN'T PAYING ATTENTION? I'LL NEVER TRUST them EVER AGAIN!" Wendy bellowed

and STARED at Mr Creeper. But Mr Creeper had NO intention of

taking the blame.

"It wasn't ME, it was WALTER – wasn't it?"

he squeaked. Walter FIERCELY denied everything.

 "Mr Creeper LET me go in! IT'S NOT MY FAULT!

IF I'd KNOWN there were snakes in those TANKS,

I'd NEVER have opened them UP! I was JUST LOOKING.

I HATE snakes!"

But everybody could see he was lying – even Wendy.

"OH. I see."  She did well to contain her FURY.

"We have to shut down the awards, Ms Wedge," Ms Hobnail repeated.

"NONSENSE! Just keep a look-out! Once I've won the award, you can do what you like. And if anyone gets bitten, just take them to hospital. They won't DIE," Wendy said.

"But … but Sally Sandal did…" Mr Creeper pointed out.

"I didn't know she'd been BITTEN. No one did until it was too late. Moving ON!"

Wendy took a step towards the stage. "Please don't, Ms Wedge!" cried Ms Hobnail.

"If you think I'm going to give UP!" shrieked Wendy, and at that, the flying shoes KICKED into ACTION.

There was nothing anyone could do to stop her.

"BACK LIVE at

THE GOLDEN

SHOE AWARDS.

Looks like we're all ready to go!

NEXT UP – it's Wendy Wedge. AND size seven is an OK size shoe

to have, just saying."

"We hear you, Kelly. THE GOLDEN SHOE AWARD

is really HOTTING up now. I think I can hear her coming

already..."

A single spotlight shone on the empty stage. Wendy was about to

make her entrance …

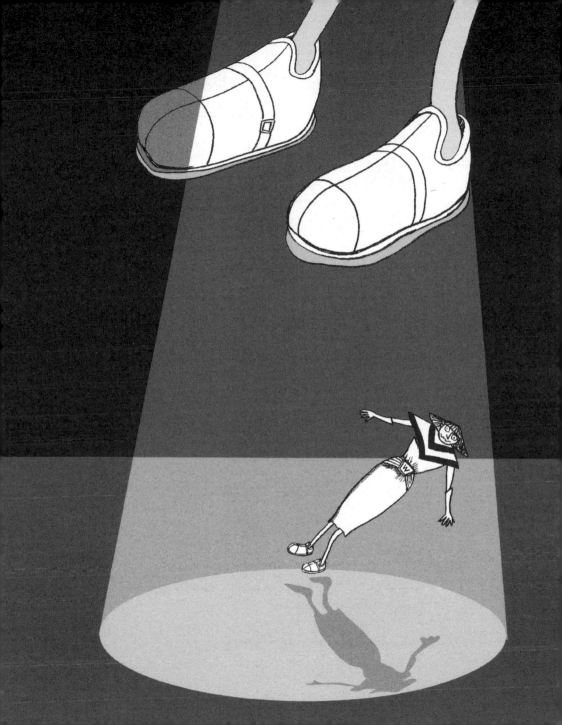

Ruby, Chelsea and Bear watched as Wendy WOBBLED her way onto the shoe stage.

"Are those the flying shoes?" Chelsea whispered.

"I think so," replied Bear.

"Why isn't she flying, then?"

Bear squinted at Wendy, who hovered for a few seconds and then dropped back down. "The wings look... stuck."

The people in the crowd weren't impressed either. They began to laugh as Wendy stumbled around.

"What's she doing?" someone yelled.

"Wendy gets the award for the dullest shoes – AGAIN!" sneered another.

There was still no sign of Betty, Bert or Dad and Ruby was starting to wonder if something had gone wrong.

"COME ON!" a man bravely shouted out.

Wendy shot him a GLARE. Then, through gritted teeth, she hissed: **"I'll show you all… SHOES UP!"**

The two wings unfolded properly and began to flutter. Wendy gradually LIFTED off the ground and the audience GASPED as she began to fly over their heads.

Ruby pulled a face. "Dad should be up there flying, not HER."

But where were the grown-ups? Time was running out.

Wendy went from side to side, upside-down and around the heads of the crowd. She even got a bit carried away and did a LOOP-THE-LOOP. Then, just when everything was going SO well, she JOLTED to one side.

Then to the other.

Oww!

Agh!

"SHOES DOWN.

SHOES DOWN!"

Wendy managed to style it out, and she floated back down and landed with a curtsey.

With the judges busy writing down notes and scores, Wendy SOAKED up the applause then STOMPED back up the shoewalk.

As soon as she got backstage, she was MORE

than delighted to see that Ms Hobnail had

arrested Betty, Bert and Ivor.

AT LAST!

"Wasn't I MARVELLOUS?" she said to them. **"You MUST**

STAY and watch me get the award. It's the LEAST I can do."

Wendy was LOVING this (too much).

"You can't hold us for ever," Ivor told her.

"That's what YOU think," Wendy snapped.

"Mother, you FLEW really well – apart from the last bit when we

ALL thought you MESSED up and Mr Creeper was laughing," said

Walter, who was a snitch.

"I wasn't," Mr Creeper said.

"You were." He was *such* a snitch.

"THE GOLDEN SHOE AWARD will be yours, Ms

Wedge," Mr Creeper reassured Wendy. At the same time he was

keeping his eyes on the ground for anything slithery.

Wendy chose to IGNORE them.

"WHEN are they going to HAND me my award?" she asked impatiently. An assistant ran up.

"Ms Wedge, the judges' scores are in. Would you like to take your place?"

"My place is NEXT to the PRIZE. I can get it faster then, before Ms Grumpy Chops over there tries to stop everything."

Wendy elbowed her way past the other contestants and casually leaned right NEXT to **THE GOLDEN SHOE AWARD.**

"WE ALL know there's only ONE winner!"

Wendy announced.

The judges tried not to be intimidated and gave out the prizes for:

Best Special Effect, Best Use of Materials, Best Sound, Most Ecological.

"For goodness' SAKE!" Wendy muttered and ROLLED her eyes.

Kelly Kitten and Peter Peeptoe had joined them now to PRESENT the winner.

"FINALLY, Kelly, we're at the main event. The award to end all awards. THIS is the moment you've all been waiting for!"

"That's right, Pete.

THE GOLDEN SHOE AWARD

this year goes to…"

"…We'll be BACK after an AD break!"

Have a GREAT holiday - but don't forget your TRAVEL INSURANCE.

Terms and conditons apply

winhahfouboffasd gho sur: hrushgowih/drwihihqohghgwngohttwuhjfgaofhiwuih guwut snasjfhiegilwru iytg whorughalwaguwdriwglEP-Be GPUSKBE HYGHEOFH FIIIHGHPG WOIEROSGRH OHEIG RFGHGIOHHPFFDIFWHW GEAIWOHPOIH OI HOPWHEORGOWIHEGOHWEGOK LEHIGOWIHEOWORGOWIHWGCAG WEBAGGOWGOYHOWENHDFNE HOPHEGIUE RGO IWUHERIWURGF IQUGSPFQOERHHAYIITWISH NHGW REIGOWIHEIWCWIBGH GIW URGIWGGGOIWEGOWEGOWIHE JOJHIGEHJP PIHHHG hrtihgfo efhohgfo fjgiojfocoppsd

"And we're back! Are you ready for a VERY special announcement?"

"GET ON WITH IT!" Wendy shrieked from the side, then remembered she was on TV.

"Someone's keen! Well, the WINNER of this year's **GOLDEN SHOE AWARD** is…

"Wendy Wedge from Wedge Town, formerly known as Shoe Town, with her amazing, incredible, never-before-seen flying shoes!"

Wendy SNATCHED **THE GOLDEN SHOE AWARD** and CLUTCHED it tightly so no one could take it away.

"AT LAST! It's mine, ALL MINE!" she cried out. Then Wendy's eyes narrowed and she made a speech.

Not a nice one either.

"It's about TIME I got this award. It's SO well deserved! I have no one to THANK but myself. BUT I have a lot of people to blame for almost SPOILING my moment. It's not been easy to concentrate. There's a bunch of people HERE we had to ARREST! Bring them OUT."

Ms Hobnail decided to ENJOY her moment of glory and shoved Bert, Betty and Ivor on to the shoewalk.

The crowd had no idea what was going on, but Ruby, Bear and Chelsea knew EXACTLY what was happening!

(It was NOW or never to show their film on the BIG screen.)

"These TERRIBLE people have been PLOTTING against ME. And they're not the ONLY ones!" Wendy spun around and GLARED into the crowd.

"Chief Inspector Slingback, ARREST those funny-looking kids. Don't think I didn't SEE you there the WHOLE time!"

Wendy said, pointing at Ruby, Bear and Chelsea. The spotlight landed on a small man with a moustache.

"NO, not HIM! THEM – YES!"

The crowd began to mutter. No one liked the idea of chasing kids.

"Listen to ME – THOSE kids are CRIMINALS. They ruined my sign and TERRORISED my son with RED paint. And this man HERE…" (She pointed to Ivor.) "… BROKE WEDGE LAW. He's been arrested for the possession of illegal SLIPPERS!"

"THESE two helped him. NO ONE IN WEDGE TOWN SHOULD OWN A PAIR OF THOSE TERRIBLE THINGS. SLIPPERS ARE BANNED! ANYONE OWNING THEM HAS TO BE ARRESTED!"

The crowd began to **LAUGH.** (A lot.)

Wendy was NOT happy at all.

At that moment, Ruby flipped on the camera, which projected the film behind Wendy. Inspector Slingback made a grab for her but Bear fended him off. Chelsea threw some sausages at the dogs, to create some extra chaos.

Look OUT!

Woof Woof!

"DID you hear me?
ILLEGAL slippers!
IT'S SHOCKING!"

Wendy shouted again, and everyone screeched with

laughter even more.

Ha!
HA! HA!
HA!
Ha!

Ha!
HA! HA!
HA!

Ha!

On the screen BEHIND Wendy Wedge were her feet wearing her pink, fluffy slippers with pom-poms. The timing couldn't have been more perfect.

"Don't LAUGH – you have NO idea WHAT they've done!" Wendy shouted back. Ivor tried to BREAK free to help his kids.

"Take your hands off my kids. YOU'RE the one in trouble," he told her bravely.

"RUBBISH! Your FERAL children vandalized my sign and dropped PAINT on to my POOR WALTER, who needs an apology NOW. Say SORRY to MY son PUBLICLY, you FOUL FOOTS," Wendy shouted, then beckoned for Walter to join her.

"Mother, I think the crowd are laughing at you," Walter had to explain to his mother as the laughing got louder.

The Shoe Police tried to GRAB the children, but they wriggled

FREE.

NOW the whole country was watching events unfold LIVE on

SHOE TIME TV.

Wendy turned then and saw the film behind her.

"It's a fake!" she screamed. **"Part**

Ruby's wig

of a terrible smear campaign!"

Ruby wasn't having any of it.

She jumped up on stage and told everyone the TRUTH.

"It's NOT FAKE! I saw her wearing slippers!" she told the

crowd. Then Bear and Chelsea joined her.

"Wendy Wedge keeps SNAKES and other

RARE creatures to make SECRET WEDGES

from. WE SAW them!" Bear added.

"RUBBISH! That's a lot of OLD shoe leather. Don't listen to

these CHILDREN!" Wendy said, forcing a smile.

Now Chelsea joined them. "LOOK, everyone – here's what Wendy keeps a secret!"

Wendy turned round and SAW for herself THE HORROR of all her SECRETS on the screen. The bugs. The snakes. The SLIPPERS.

"STOP THAT FAKE FILM RIGHT NOW! HOW did this happen?" Wendy looked at Ms Hobnail – and around desperately for Mr Creeper too.

"THOSE snakes on the loose are poisonous, and they are the SAME snakes that bit and KILLED my Sally Sandal!" Ivor told Wendy angrily.

"It wasn't MY fault a SNAKE escaped! Sally was in the WRONG place at the WRONG time. So NOT my fault. AND those kids FAKED that film! It's a load of old FOOTSWALLOP, isn't it, Chief Inspector Slingback? And Mr Creeper, you'll stick up for me?"

But there was no answer. Desperately,

Wendy tried to FLY AWAY.

"Not so fast!" Ivor shouted and tried

to GRAB her foot, but she slipped AWAY!

OFF she flew over everyone's heads, trying hard to keep hold of

her **GOLDEN SHOE AWARD.** (Which wasn't easy.)

Ruby, Bear, Chelsea, Ivor, Betty and Bert watched her helplessly

from the stage. She was getting away with it!

Then, out of NOWHERE

from the crowd, a thin rope SHOT out

and wrapped around Wendy's ankles, tying them together.

Then like a FISH on a hook, she was dragged down to the ground.

"GERRROFF ME!" she yelped.

The crowd parted and at the END of the rope, pulling Wendy

Wedge to the ground, was ...

... MRS COURT!

"Is that YOU, Mrs Court?" Ruby gasped.

Bear and Chelsea had their mouths

open in amazement.

Mrs Court ignored them.
She calmly finished pulling
Wendy Wedge to earth with her
special walking stick.

Wendy looked surprised to be
rumbled as well. Then, a group
of official-looking
police stepped
onto the stage.

"WHAT do you think you're DOING?" Wendy shouted.

"WENDY WEDGE, MY NAME IS CYBIL COURT, and I'M

FROM THE FEDERAL FOOTWEAR INVESTIGATIONS TEAM.

YOU ARE UNDER ARREST FOR SO MANY THINGS I HARDLY

KNOW WHERE TO BEGIN. So let's start with THESE:

1. USING RARE, PROTECTED CREATURES

     TO MAKE WEDGES.

2. ILLEGALLY KEEPING POISONOUS SNAKES.

3. NOT KEEPING YOUR SNAKES SECURE

     so they escaped and killed Sally Sandal.

4. MAKING UP YOUR OWN LAWS. There's

     NOTHING wrong with SLIPPERS.

5. KIDNAPPING YOUR WORKERS and

     threatening CHILDREN.

6. NOT PAYING YOUR TAXES.

I COULD GO ON."

Mrs Court sent her officers out to arrest Chief Inspector Slingback too, for taking BRIBES from Wendy and generally being a RUBBISH inspector.

Mrs Court turned to Ivor. "I've been WATCHING your house for some time, Mr Foot, as part of my wider investigation into Ms Wedge. I saw the flying shoes, I warned off Mr Creeper with my special DART blower, and I wanted to keep your flying shoes safe for you, so I TOOK them before Mr Creeper had a chance. HERE they are, Mr Foot."

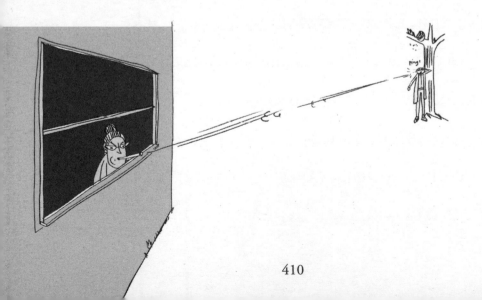

She took them out of her bag and passed them over.

"Mrs Court? YOU had them!" Ivor said, gratefully taking back Sally's shoes.

"Mrs Court has saved the day!" Bear cheered.

"HOORAY for Mrs Court!" Ruby yelled, pleased to have an opportunity to admire her walking stick at close range.

"This belongs to you, too," Mrs Court said, handing Sally Sandal's book to Ruby and Bear. "Look after it. It's clearly something VERY special. I wouldn't mind wearing a few of those shoes, IF you ever make them."

Ruby, Bear and Chelsea were speechless. NOSY old Mrs Court

was the last person they expected to SAVE the day.

Bert walked up on stage and TOOK the shoes off Wendy.

"Officers, and the Shoe Award Jury,

I think you'll ALSO find Wendy

Wedge STOLE these shoes from ME.

They are the creation of the wonderful

Sally Sandal."

Wendy knew the GAME was up, so she tried another tactic.

"All I've ever tried to DO was be nice to people, GIVE

everyone a JOB, and look after everyone in WEDGE— um,

Shoe Town. ASK Mr Creeper! HE's about to get a BIG

promotion. MR CREEPER, you can tell them how kind

I am, can't you?"

If Wendy THOUGHT Mr Creeper was going to STICK up for her, she was WRONG.

Mr Creeper stepped forwards. "Wendy has done ALL the things you accuse her of. I'm ashamed to say I've helped her. I can give you all the evidence you need. I'd rather see those creatures FREE in the wild than on someone's FEET."

He then turned to Wendy. "I'm tired of being treated badly, Ms Wedge. You've been an absolute nightmare to work for."

(And that was an understatement.)

Wendy was SHOCKED.

"AND you need to say NO to your son once in a while and READ stories to him a lot more."

Mr Creeper finished his speech and felt nothing but RELIEF!

"Mother, what's going to happen to ME now? Because I WOULD quite like to have stories read to me," Walter piped up.

"Well that's not going to happen now, IS it?" Wendy snapped at her son as she was dragged away by the police. **"I'll instruct MY lawyers to get me out. In the meantime, your Uncle Wilberforce Wedge will have to look after you."**

"BUT I hardly KNOW him," Walter whinged.

"What's to know? He was our parents' favourite child. He always laughed at me, made me feel useless, blah blah. He'll look after you. He can't make you WORSE than you already are."

"MOTHER, how can you say that?" Walter cried.

"Mr Creeper's right. I should have said 'no' to you more. So, I'll start now. Can you stay with someone else? NO! TOUGH."

Wendy thought she'd try ONE last thing to get RID of all these annoying people around her.

She called HER DOGS.

"LEFT and RIGHT, GET me out of here! SEIZE them!"

The dogs glanced up, but they didn't feel like moving much. Not after all those sausages.

Wendy sighed. It was all over.

One of the judges tried to wrestle **THE GOLDEN SHOE AWARD** away from her.

"BUT that's mine! I won it – you GAVE it to me!" she wailed.

"Not any more, Wendy Wedge. We're awarding it to Bert Brogue who MADE the flying shoes."

Bert came up to take it and turned to the cameras. "Thank you. BUT this doesn't belong to me, it belongs to Ivor, Ruby and Bear Foot and to their mother, Sally Sandal, who designed the shoes. I just followed her instructions."

Bert handed the award to the Foot Family.

They were all smiling for the cameras and celebrating when

someone in the crowd shouted...

"SNAKE! SNAKE!"

Which wasn't an insult aimed at Wendy BUT THE REAL

THING!

AGGHHHHHHHHH!

There was MAD PANIC as everyone ran in all different

directions. The snake was slithering UP the shoewalk – right

towards the stage!

IVOR FROZE. He had a deep-seated FEAR of snakes.

Bert threw his shoe at it, which only

made it MADDER.

Then Ruby sP**RANG** into action.

She GRABBED Mrs Court's walking stick and pointed it at the snake, while pressing ALL the buttons. A SHARP FORK shot out of the top and PINNED the snake down.

"Don't go near it!" Mrs Court shouted.

The snake was starting to work its way

OUT of the prong, when suddenly

Shoo the cat appeared from

backstage and POUNCED on it.

Shoo held it down long enough for Officer Slingback and Officer Trainer to arrive with a BIG **shoebox** and take it away safely.

The crowd began to cheer and clap their hands in relief.

Size Thirty-Five

"It's been QUITE a show! We've had flying shoes – those were A

M A Z I N G. I want a pair of those right now! Don't you, Pete?"

"I really do, Kelly. What I don't want to see again is a

SNAKE. Here are the WINNERS of

THE GOLDEN SHOE AWARD to tell us all about

what happened today.

"Ivor, what can you tell us? Ivor?"

"Hi, I'm Ruby. Dad's in SHOCK right now. He doesn't like snakes.

This is my friend, Chelsea. She lives next door."

"Hi! My mum's over there. Her name's Betty and she rescued Ruby and Bear when Wendy was after them. We had a sleepover – and I gave them Mum's pass to get into World of Wedge," Chelsea said.

"She did and THAT helped us get into the secret place where the CREATURES were. AND this is my brother, Bear."

"Hi! My sister talks a lot. THAT'S Bert. He MADE the shoes from a book that our mum wrote. Bert, come and say hello."

"Bert, you must be proud of making the shoes too?"

Kelly Kitten asked.

"Well, it's really Sally and Ivor's dream. I hope we can make more and sell them in MY shop – Bert's Brogues – which will be staying OPEN FOR EVER now!" Bert said and did a little dance on live TV.

Then Ivor warmed up and joined in and so did Betty and the kids too.

"What a happy ending to a VERY eventful day. The judges awarded **THE GOLDEN SHOE AWARD** to Ivor Foot and Sally Sandal in the end. So let's leave you with the whole FOOT family and friends dancing!"

"Until next year! It's Kelly Kitten and Peter Peeptoe saying BYE for now from Wedge Town – I mean **SHOE TOWN!**"

Keep smiling.

"Hey, Bear ... do you think Mum would like my shoe shuffle dance?" Ruby wanted to know.

"She'd love it!" Bear said.

"Your mum would be very proud of us all…" Dad added and gave them a hug. "It's all in the foot action, kids – see?" he added and joined in.

So, I know what you're wondering now...

What happened after Wendy was dragged to Shoe Prison?

Left and Right went to live with Mr Creeper who, in

exchange for giving evidence against

Wendy, was given a suspended sentence,

after completing some

community service picking

up litter.

Mrs Court's walking stick

came in very handy for that.

He eventually got to go on a well-earned holiday.

(The dogs went too.)

Walter was sent to stay with Wendy's brother, Wilberforce Wedge, who had refused to come to **Shoe Town** to look after him.

(The truth was HE had been in prison for years. He was let out for good

behaviour just as Wendy arrived, but that's another story.)

Bert kept his shop open and started to make flying brogues.

The World of Wedge was renamed WOOF, World Of Original Footwear. Betty and Ivor took over design and production at WOOF. They created and sold the type of weird and wonderful shoes that Ivor and Sally used to make in their shop, using many of Sally Sandal's original designs. Some of the money from the shoes went to look after the RARE creatures and bugs and keep them safe. Even the snakes.

WOOF did SO well that all the **shoebox** houses were able to have MORE storeys put on top of them so they weren't so tiny any more.

Ruby and Bear got their OWN ROOMS, which stopped them from arguing about who was the messiest. There was more space, which meant Chelsea could come for sleepovers as well.

Bear still liked tinned peaches with lemon curd and was writing a lot of stories himself now. He already had plenty of material to work with (his family's war with Wendy for a start).

Ruby had a go at making a walking stick like Cybil Court's. Hers was painted with lightning bolts and she mostly used it to annoy Bear.

Pretty much everything was going well.

There were a few problems at first with people FLYING all over the place but after a while they got used to sticking to certain RULES in the air so everyone could be safe.

And flying shoes really are as fun as they look.

You'll never be late for school again. (Ever!)

You can see over TALL people's heads.

(No problem at all.)

You can reach for stuff that's up high. (Easy peasy.)

AND if you ever get chased UP a tree by a dog again – DON'T PANIC.

Escaping couldn't be simpler (and it beats climbing a tree).

Wendy was allowed a few home comforts in Shoe Prison.

Meanwhile...

Wilberforce Wedge on holiday was enjoying the

news of his gruesome twin sister's downfall

(a bit too much.)

**SHOO – DOING
THE SHOE SHUFFLE**

Liz Pichon is one of the UK's best-loved and bestselling creators of children's books. Her TOM GATES  series has been translated into 45 languages, sold millions of copies worldwide, and has won the Roald Dahl Funny Prize, the Blue Peter Book Award for Best Story and the younger fiction category of the Waterstones Children's Book Prize.

In the ten years since THE BRILLIANT WORLD OF TOM GATES first published, the books have inspired the nation's children to get creative, whether that's through reading, drawing, doodling, writing, making, music or performing.

"I wanted to FILL the books with ALL the things I loved doing when I was a kid. It's just the best feeling ever to know children are enjoying reading the books, because I love making them. So thank you so much for choosing Tom Gates and keep reading and doodling!"

Keep up to date at lizpichon.com

Over to you Liz Pichon...

Make it snappy, it's been a long book.

OK, here goes... (I've got a lot of people to thank). Firstly HUGE thanks to my publishers Scholastic, who have worked so hard to put this book together. Catherine Bell, Miriam Farbey and Dick Robinson. To my brilliant editors, thank you for your patience and expert EYES: Sam Smith, Lauren Fortune, Abigail McAden, Genevieve Herr and Pete Matthews. To the fabulous art folk: Andrew Biscomb, Jason Cox and my sister Lyn (who came to the rescue as ever!). Thanks to Hannah Love, Penelope Daukes, Toni Pelari, Claire Tagg and all the team for getting the book OUT into the world. MASSIVE thanks to my wonderful agent (of over 20 years), Caroline Walsh. BIG love to my family, who put up with me during my deadlines. Mark, Zak, Ella and Lily – I love you loads xxxxxxx

Keep your BEADY EYES open for the hilarious TOM GATES books!

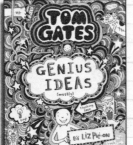

For more news about Liz Pichon and the Tom Gates books, go to: Lizpichon.com
AND to Scholastic's fantastic Tom Gates website: thebrilliantworldoftomgates.com

So many books

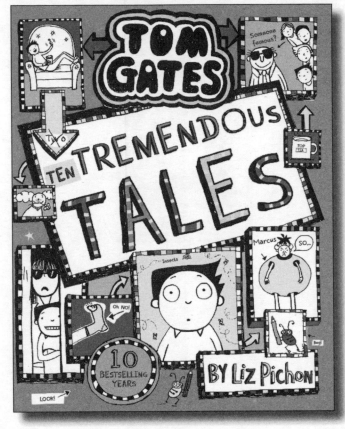

Don't miss this laugh-out-loud, fully illustrated collection of stories starring **Tom Gates** and his friends, family and foes!